"You're still not s... marrying me?"

She bestowed a deep blue enigmatic gaze on him. "What do you expect, Etienne? I may have enjoyed kissing you, but that's a far cry from—" she hesitated "—from…"

"Laying down all your arms?" he suggested.

"I would like to know…" She stopped and cleared her throat. "I would like to know if I'm expected to go to bed with you tonight? I mean I know, and accept, that it has to happen sometime, but—" She stopped again.

"I shouldn't take it as an indication that you're ready to leap into bed with me?" He reached over to take her hand and fiddled with his wedding ring. "Am I correct in assuming that you're a virgin, Mel?"

Some of our bestselling writers are Australians!

Lindsay Armstrong…
Helen Bianchin…
Emma Darcy…
Miranda Lee…

Look out for their novels about the
Wonder from Down Under—
where spirited women win the hearts of
Australia's most eligible men.

THE AUSTRALIANS

He's big, he's brash, he's brazen—he's Australian!

Coming soon:

The Billionaire's Contract Bride
by
Carol Marinelli
#2372

Lindsay Armstrong

THE UNCONVENTIONAL BRIDE

THE AUSTRALIANS

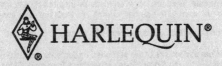

HARLEQUIN®

TORONTO • NEW YORK • LONDON
AMSTERDAM • PARIS • SYDNEY • HAMBURG
STOCKHOLM • ATHENS • TOKYO • MILAN • MADRID
PRAGUE • WARSAW • BUDAPEST • AUCKLAND

ISBN 0-373-12359-0

THE UNCONVENTIONAL BRIDE

First North American Publication 2003.

Copyright © 2003 by Lindsay Armstrong.

CHAPTER ONE

ETIENNE Hurst stood in the cold wind of a grey winter's day and was amazed to find himself stirred by a woman.

A girl, more accurately, he reflected, and one who had little time for him although he hadn't seen her for over a year. Had that changed, though, he wondered, changed as she had changed? She would be...nineteen now, he estimated. All grown up, but who would have guessed Melinda Ethridge would grow into this willowy creature, this fascinating, haunting figure, as she farewelled her father and stepmother, who'd been killed in a light-plane crash?

Standing quite still, dressed in black but with her wonderful chestnut hair uncovered, she seemed to be in a world of her own. She wasn't crying, although there was deep sorrow stamped into the young, pale oval of her face and the pure line of her throat was essentially vulnerable. Nevertheless, her tall, slender figure was erect, even proud, as the wind swirled her long black skirt around her legs and lifted her hair.

Of course, women had stirred him before, he thought rather grimly. There couldn't be a stranger time for it, however, than while he was making his own farewells to his older sister, Margot, who had been Melinda's stepmother. Nor could there be much reason to it. Melinda, universally known as Mel, had never got on with her stepmother and, by implication, had included the other member of the Hurst family under the umbrella of her dislike.

However, there was even less reason to it from the point of view that she was so young. At thirty himself, he thought he'd grown out of bright, breathless young things who fell madly in love at the drop of a hat. On top of that—he paused a moment to think of his sister, Margot. She had married Mel's father four years ago and brought glamour, sophistication and an expensive lifestyle to Raspberry Hill, the Ethridge family property, but at what cost? he wondered.

In other words, if, as he suspected, his beautiful, social-butterfly sister had stretched the family finances to the limit, what lay before Mel Ethridge and her three younger brothers and how much of it was his responsibility?

All the more reason to ignore this sudden fire in his loins, he reasoned with some well-placed irony.

Then she looked up and across at him and her eyes were like deep blue velvet. He saw recognition come to them, saw them widen and stay wide and trapped beneath his gaze until she blinked suddenly and accorded him a grave nod. And he knew he'd been unable to take his own advice in regard to this girl, although she turned to her brothers without a word and began to shepherd them to the waiting cars.

CHAPTER TWO

THREE weeks later, Mel Ethridge was driving a tractor to the storage shed with a load of pineapples in the trailer. It was a pleasant, sunny morning, spring had sprung, and she was feeling a bit better to be out and about and working on Raspberry Hill.

It had been a tough three weeks in more ways than one. Not only had she lost a beloved parent but she'd also made the discovery that Raspberry Hill, a mixed property that grew pineapples and ran fat cattle and was the only home she'd known, was in dire financial straits.

Then she noticed a familiar car, sleek, silver and shining, parked beside the shed—Etienne Hurst's car.

She sighed but there was no help for it. Etienne was leaning against the car and it was obvious she'd seen him and been seen. Nor was it the first time she'd seen him since the funeral, although prior to it it had been some time. He'd also been out of the country at the time of the accident and had only just got home in time for the funeral.

Since then, as his sister's next of kin, he'd been present at the reading of the wills, and he knew as well as she did how precarious the situation was. Not only that, if you didn't dislike him, you had to admit he'd gone out of his way to be helpful to the orphaned Ethridge family.

The problem was, she did dislike him.

7

She'd resented his sister, who'd married her widowed father out of the blue four years ago and been the root cause of a lot of her problems, and she resented Etienne accordingly; well, that was more or less the scenario.

She brought the tractor to a halt and jumped down. 'Good day!' She stripped off her gloves. 'What can I do for you, Etienne?'

His dark gaze roamed over her dusty jeans, her grease-stained shirt and the bright cotton scarf covering her hair. None of it diminished the slip and flow of a lovely, active figure, the bloom of youth and those amazing eyes.

'Just came to see how it was going. Good crop this year?' He gestured to the pineapples.

'Not bad; we've had better, but not bad. Quality is good but,' she tipped a hand, 'quantity is down.' She hauled a pine complete with spiky crown out of the trailer and presented it to him. 'Take it home; it should be sweet and juicy.'

He weighed it in his hand then placed it on the bonnet. 'Thanks. How are the cattle going?'

Mel wrinkled her nose. 'I'm a bit worried about the feed; we didn't get as much winter rain as we needed but,' she shrugged, 'time will tell.'

He grinned. 'You know what they say about farmers, Mel?'

She shook her head.

'They're always complaining.'

Mel folded her arms and studied him comprehensively. He had dark, curly hair and dark eyes, and stamped into his long lines there was not only strength but also magnificent coordination combined with the ability to be very still but supremely alert. An almost hunter-like quality, she'd thought several times, even though he also possessed an easy charm.

Although the more you got know him, the more you began to suspect it didn't quite hide a cool determination to get his own way. Being possessed of the same trait, a liking for her own way, was not, she foresaw, going to help her in her dealings with him.

She moved at last. 'You should try it yourself, then you might understand why.'

'Sorry, only joking,' he murmured, instantly causing her to feel humourless and pretentious.

To counter it and show him she knew what she was talking about, she offered him a tour of the property.

'I'd like that—my car or yours?'

She glanced at his clean jeans and pressed short-sleeved blue cotton shirt with flap pockets, then down at herself and finally over to the battered ute she drove. 'Uh—perhaps we should walk. You're too clean for my ute and I'm too dirty for your car.'

'That's fine with me, although I could put a rug over the seat for you—'

'No. We'll walk! Now, first of all,' she led the way down a path behind the shed, 'from this little rise you can see the cattle paddocks. Naturally, we rotate them and improve them, so those on the left are "resting" at the moment and,' she swung her arm, 'over there you see the herd.'

'How many head?'

'About a hundred.'

He said nothing for a moment then stated a figure in dollars.

Mel glanced up at him in surprise because it was a pretty accurate estimate of how much the herd represented to Raspberry Hill in financial terms. 'You've been doing some homework?'

He nodded.

She waited but he said no more so she walked him through a pineapple paddock, showed him the stables where Rimfire, her horse, whickered affectionately and accepted some cube sugar she always kept in her pocket. Then she took him on to her pet project, free-range chickens. Not that she sold the chickens, only the eggs. This time he put some surprisingly astute questions on the cost-profit ratio of the project to her.

'It's not that profitable yet,' she told him, 'but to be quite honest I don't care if it never is. I'm passionate about the abolition of battery hens.'

He looked at her keenly. 'I believe there are a few things you're passionate about.'

'Well, yes, I guess there are,' she conceded. 'I can't abide cruelty to animals, or anyone, so I'm a paid-up member of Amnesty International and I raise money for the RSPCA. And since I began to worry about the environment I've joined Greenpeace.'

Etienne Hurst's first instinct was amusement but they were leaning side by side against the fence watching her flock of chickens, and she was so unconsciously lovely in her very serious defence of so much his next sentiment was affection.

All the same, he cautioned himself, do-gooders, especially if they didn't have a sense of humour, could be hard work at times.

Then he frowned at another thought. 'How come you seem to run the whole farm, Mel?'

'When I left school it was all I wanted to do,' she answered. 'So I persuaded Dad to let me help and as he and Margot began to travel more and more I—took over more and more. But...' She paused.

'Go on,' he invited.

'Well, I guess it was becoming obvious we needed an injection of cash for fence improvements, a new dam, a new tractor and so on, but Dad kept deferring it all.'

'For which you blame me?' he suggested.

Mel took a breath. 'Not at all.'

'Then why do I get the impression you view me along with cane toads and other undesirables?'

Mel coloured and bit her lip.

'I know you didn't get on with Margot but I fail to see what that has to do with me,' he said. 'Especially now.'

'I don't like to say this because I'm sure you're grieving as much as I am, Etienne, but, since you brought it up, Raspberry Hill started to go downhill from the time Dad married Margot.'

'She made him happy,' he pointed out. And when Mel looked uncomfortable, he added, 'There were also other factors involved. Investments that didn't turn out well, for example, but I admit that Margot always had expensive tastes.'

Mel watched her busy chickens, heads down and bottoms up, as they enjoyed their large, grassy run and all the choice titbits it offered. Then she turned and looked towards the homestead, situated on a headland that overlooked the waters of the Curtis Coast and, from this angle, silhouetted against the skyline. It was a sprawling old wooden Queenslander beneath a green tin roof, and now, thanks to Etienne's sister, it was fully restored and a treasure trove of antiques, whereas before it had been a big, untidy but comfortable family home.

But was it fair to transfer her animosity to Margot's brother? she wondered. And why was she conscious of a feeling of being at sixes and sevens in his company—aware of him—in a way that didn't often happen to her?

Was it just the usual effect he had on the opposite sex?

'Uh—she certainly had marvellous taste,' she said by way of turning aside her thoughts about Etienne Hurst as a man as well as not wishing to speak ill of the dead and regretting her earlier comments on his sister. 'Anyway, I don't think there's much more I can show you, Etienne, but—' She stopped on a sudden thought. 'If there's anything from the house you'd like as a memento of Margot—would you like to come up and have a look?'

He considered. 'There is a miniature of our mother—'

'Oh, I know it! It's still on the dresser in their bedroom. Let's go up now.'

This time he wouldn't take no for an answer and insisted on driving her to the house in his car. Mrs Bedwell, who had been the housekeeper at Raspberry Hill for as long as Mel could remember, came out to greet them.

'Just in time for lunch,' Mrs Bedwell enthused. 'I've set the table here on the veranda.'

'But,' Mel bit her tongue, 'I mean, I'm not sure if Etienne has time for lunch—'

'Of course he does!' Mrs Bedwell resembled a tall, grey but colourfully attired stork and was renowned for her meddling. 'Now, you just sit down, Mr Hurst—how about a beer? It's such a lovely, hot day! I'll get you one and that will give Mel a chance to duck under the shower.'

Mel opened and closed her mouth as Etienne replied that he could do with a beer, thank you very much, and Mrs Bedwell caught her wrist and steered her inside.

'Will you stop pushing me around?' she said to Mrs Bedwell once they were out of earshot. 'And how can you give him lunch when you've only just laid eyes on him, and how about consulting me first before you issue invitations left, right and centre?'

'How? It's simple—I saw him drive in, I give you lunch every day and if you think I can't stretch it to two you don't know me very well, Mel! As for issuing invitations left, right and centre, I just knew it would never cross your mind to do it so I figured I might as well do it for you. You've got ten minutes!'

'But *why* do we need him to come to lunch?' Mel protested.

Mrs Bedwell put her hands on her hips. 'Only you could be so thick, Mel. Now, you just do as you're told and make sure you're nice to him!'

Mel regarded Mrs Bedwell's retreating back with smouldering eyes despite the fact that she was extremely fond of her, then she shrugged and went to shower.

Fifteen minutes later, she came out onto the veranda in clean jeans and a floral blouse and carrying the miniature carefully wrapped up in tissue paper. She'd run the gauntlet of Mrs Bedwell again, to be asked in exasperated tones why she couldn't have worn a dress, and had answered simply that it hadn't crossed her mind.

'Sorry,' she sat down opposite Etienne, who rose briefly, 'to have left you alone like this but Mrs Bedwell is a stickler for the niceties.'

He looked at his watch then took in her appearance. All the dust and grease had disappeared. Her hair, released from the scarf, rippled and glinted like new pennies in a well-brushed loose cascade to her shoulders and her skin was smooth and fresh.

'I was prepared for at least half an hour, so you did well.' He reached for his beer but for some reason their gazes locked.

Something trickled along Mel's nerve-endings as she couldn't look away, a strange little *frisson* that made her feel excited but also vulnerable and somehow at the mercy of this man.

Then he cut the eye contact but not before Mel remembered the look she'd intercepted from him three weeks earlier. A look that, in the most surprising circumstances, had held her trapped at the sheer unexpectedness of it. It came back to her now, and left her posing a question to herself.

For the first time since she'd known him, was Etienne Hurst looking at her as a woman rather than a troublesome tomboy who'd always made it clear she didn't like him? But, perhaps more pertinently, was she responding in kind to it?

'How are the boys?'

She blinked and tried to deal with the change of

subject smoothly as she thought of her three brothers, Justin, Ewan and Tosh, aged fifteen, twelve and ten respectively. 'As well as can be expected. Still lost and bewildered. Tosh was having nightmares so I got him a puppy.' She grimaced.

Tosh, short for Thomas, which Ewan hadn't been able to pronounce so the baby name of Tosh had stuck, had been allowed to choose his puppy. The result was a three-month-old tan and white Jack Russell he'd named Batman, who was almost as mischievous and trouble-prone as his new owner. Although, since Batman had been allowed to sleep on Tosh's bed, the nightmares had stopped.

'Talking of Batman,' Mel added as Mrs Bedwell came on the veranda pushing a trolley, 'where is the little monster?'

Mrs Bedwell laid before them a minor feast. Cold chicken and ham, a green salad, her home-grown and cooked beetroot, new potatoes in their jackets sprinkled with parsley and drizzled with garlic butter and warm crusty rolls. 'That dratted dog,' she intoned, 'is asleep, thank the lord!'

'What's he done this morning?' Mel asked with resignation.

'You wouldn't want to know! There.' Mrs Bedwell stood back. 'Enjoy your lunch!'

The smile of thanks Etienne Hurst bestowed on her was dazzling and she retreated indoors in some disarray, causing Mel to think darkly that she resented being included in the universal effect on women this man had, however, well, slightly intoxicating it was.

'So you're not working today, Etienne?' she queried as they started their lunch.

'I am. I'm just taking a few hours off to make sure you're coping, Mel.'

She broke open a roll and buttered it. 'It's going to be a bit of a battle, obviously, but—'

'It's going to be an uphill battle, Mel,' he broke in, 'let's not beat about the bush. All your profits are going to go in repaying the mortgage on Raspberry Hill.'

She looked up, deep concern in her blue eyes. 'Surely not. I mean, I can't believe Dad would have let it get to this stage.'

'Mel, as I probably don't need to tell you, seasonal irregularities have made pineapples a dicey crop at the moment. Raspberry Hill would not have been the only property affected—it's why more and more people have diversified. So it wasn't so much that your father "let it get to this stage". If anything the weather has been the problem or at least a significant part of it.'

She said nothing.

He put his knife and fork down. 'But things having happened the way they have may mean that you have to face the fact that you won't be able to save Raspberry Hill.'

Mel said huskily, 'I can't believe that. We all love it so much, the boys as much as I do.'

'They…they're young, Mel,' he said.

'Young enough to get over it? I don't know. It's also a unifying factor in our lives and our *heritage*.' She stared at her plate with deep distress then pushed it impatiently away half-finished. 'I will not,' the distress was suddenly replaced with determination, 'give up, Etienne. Whatever it takes to save Raspberry Hill I will do.'

'Such as?'

The question came with businesslike precision.

'I may have to subdivide it. That's one thing I've been thinking of,' she said slowly.

'It's a possibility,' he agreed. 'But then you face the prospect of a smaller holding being unviable.'

Mel swallowed hard. 'Maybe a guest farm? I think there's a market for real country experience holidays.'

Something in his dark gaze softened but he didn't respond.

'What's so silly about that?' she asked tartly.

'It's not that it's silly but you'd need capital to start it off.'

'A lot of misguided capital has been spent on this house,' she said.

'I take your point,' he replied evenly, 'but it may not be that easy to realise. There's also the problem of who is going to stand *in loco parentis* of three young boys.'

Mel was crumbling what was left of her roll into tiny pieces as she struggled with perhaps the greatest of her problems, when a ball of white and tan fur erupted onto the veranda and Batman leapt onto her lap. He licked her face profusely, knocked her side-plate off the table then leapt down to do an ecstatic jig along the floorboards.

Mrs Bedwell arrived hot on his heels and scooped him up in her arms. 'You little wretch! As if I haven't got enough to do without babysitting you—why on earth didn't that plate break?'

Etienne got up. 'Here, I'll take him. Whoa!' he said

as the dog was put in his arms. 'No licking, mate!' He sat down with him and Batman subsided with an ecstatic expression as he was scratched behind his ears.

'You like dogs?' Mel asked, still blinking at the whirlwind events that had just overtaken her.

'Sure. I even had one of these as a kid. He was also as mad as a hatter but very loyal.'

She frowned. 'I can't picture that.'

'Me or the dog?'

'Uh—you.'

'You assumed I came into the world all grown up?'

'Truth to tell, since you had a French mother and both have—had—French names,' she amended, 'I've always associated you with an exotic background rather than a kid with a dog. I know Margot was born in Vanuatu.'

'She was but I was born right here in Gladstone, and other than for the name,' he looked humorous for a moment, 'I escaped a lot of the exotic influence our French mother exerted on Margot. Our father was a fair-dinkum Aussie.'

'You certainly sound like one. While she was certainly the essence of chic,' Mel murmured and frowned again. 'If you don't mind me saying so, you didn't seem to be very close. Although, of course, I could be quite wrong—but we didn't see much of you at Raspberry Hill at all.'

He stared into a space for a moment, then down at the contented dog in his arms. 'No, we weren't that close. She was ten years older, which is quite a gap, but I guess the other reason is that my business has really expanded in the last five or six years so I've had my nose to the grindstone a lot.'

'Hurst Engineering & Shipping,' Mel said. 'I don't know about having your nose to the grindstone—I once heard Margot put it as "empire building".'

He shrugged and looked amused.

'Not only Margot. Even Justin is impressed,' she added.

'As a matter of fact, he came to see me about getting a part-time job last week.'

Mel's eyes widened. 'He didn't tell me that!'

'He—er—never shared your dislike, mistrust or whatever it was of me.'

Mel coloured but it was true. Despite their initial opposition to sharing their father with a stepmother, none of the boys, for that matter, had continued their resentment of Margot nor applied it to Etienne. None of them had realised how the property was going downhill either, she reminded herself drily.

'Did you give him a job?'

'I told him I would have one for him in the next school holidays, with your approval.'

'That's very good of you,' Mel said.

'Getting back to the boys,' Etienne said, I—'

Mel scraped back her chair and stood up. 'Etienne, I appreciate your concern but it's really not your problem.'

Batman pricked up his ears.

Etienne looked down at him then up at Mel. Her expression was one of pride and dignity and it came to him that she could be exasperating at times. It also came to him that in some respects she'd led a very sheltered life, cocooned amongst her family and on

Raspberry Hill, and might be less worldly than a lot of girls of her age.

Yet, contrary to what he'd expected, the attraction he'd experienced the day of the funeral was still there. Even looking so proud and unreasonably stubborn, she stirred him. The line of her throat fascinated him. The way she squared her shoulders, always a preliminary to saying something designed to tell him he wasn't liked or trusted even if not in so many words, drew his attention to the curves of her breasts, the narrowness of her waist and the flare of her hips.

Was she at all aware of the effect she had on him, though? he wondered. What would her reaction be if he revealed his preoccupation with her figure?

'OK,' he said, ostensibly to the dog. 'I rest my case—for the time being. But if you need me, just let me know.'

'I will,' Mel agreed.

'And now I really must go,' he said politely but with a glint in his eye that indicated to her he knew she was barely able to wait to get rid of him. 'Thank you for your hospitality,' he added, by way, she was quite sure, of adding salt to the wound.

'I'll pass your thanks on to Mrs Bedwell. It was all her doing,' she replied with excessive politeness of her own.

He put Batman down and got up. 'Don't do anything I wouldn't, Mel,' he said softly.

Although she was five feet eight, he was a head taller, which put her at a disadvantage she rarely suffered. It didn't stop her from saying haughtily, however, 'Such as?' as if it was inconceivable she should do anything she might regret.

But as he took his time about answering she realised her heart was beating a little erratically and that strange mixture of excitement and wariness was coursing through her veins again. Why? she wondered. How could he, just by looking at her in a certain way, produce this result in her?

He wasn't even looking at her in that certain way right now, not as if he had her trapped in his sights as a woman to ponder about. If anything, he was looking down at her with lazy amusement, which didn't, most unfairly, stop her new awareness of him flooding her.

'Such as kicking the dog,' he said softly.

'I've never kicked a dog in my life!'

'You just had that look about you. But there's no reason to be incensed over anything,' he raised an eyebrow, 'that I know of.'

· She set her teeth then unset them. 'Goodbye, Etienne.'

'*Au revoir*, Mel; not quite the same thing.'

CHAPTER THREE

'YOU didn't tell me you'd asked Etienne for a job in your holidays, Justin.'

'I was going to present it to you as a *fait accompli*.'

The two younger boys were in bed and Mel and Justin were watching television in the den, the one room in the house that had escaped Margot's make-over. The one room where you didn't have to be careful of the furniture, could eat snacks and drink drinks with impunity and no one cared if you put your feet up on the battered old leather couch.

'Why? I mean, why couldn't you have told me?'

Justin was tall for his age, exceedingly bright and he had Mel's blue eyes and chestnut hair. He flicked the remote and changed the channel, causing his sister to grit her teeth.

'You're not always reasonable on the subject of the Hurst family, beloved,' he said, and went on flicking through the channels.

Mel grabbed the remote from him and switched the television off.

'See what I mean?' Justin offered.

'That had nothing to do with the Hursts,' she denied. 'I can't stand the way you switch from programme to programme!'

'Only to avoid the ads.'

'I like the ads; well, not precisely but,' she looked heavenwards, 'whatever, can we just talk?'

'OK. It occurred to me that we have a few financial problems and that, as the oldest male, I should try and buck in and help.'

'Fair enough,' Mel said slowly, 'but why Etienne?'

'You may not know this, Mel, but he's very successful. He took advantage of Gladstone being the largest port in Queensland and the fourth largest in the country to build up a marine-engineering works and a shipping agency.'

'Granted,' she said slowly.

Despite only being a medium-sized town in a rural area, the port of Gladstone handled millions of tonnes of coal, bauxite, alumina and other minerals and substances. It offered a deep-water port protected by close offshore islands, it was only ten or twelve days' distance from the Asia Pacific region and was endowed with plenty of energy resources—water, coal and natural gas.

'But still—why Etienne?' she asked.

Justin looked at her ironically. 'How many other millionaires do we know, Mel? Not only that but he's also almost part of the family.'

Mel opened her mouth to deny this but closed it immediately.

'How bad are things, Mel?' Justin said into the silence.

'Not good,' she conceded.

'Mrs B told me he came to lunch today.'

'Mrs B invited him to lunch—well, he did come out to see how we were going.'

'I never could work out what you've got against him!'

'You're not a girl,' she retorted.

'Plenty of girls find him irresistible, so I hear—is

that it?' Justin enquired. 'Don't tell me you've always had a crush on him!'

'I have not,' Mel contradicted. 'And from what I've heard they're not precisely girls either.'

'Women, then,' Justin said, 'or whatever the technical term is. What have you heard?'

She shrugged. 'You know that lighthouse he's leased and renovated? Apparently there's been a stream of gorgeous, sophisticated, definitely women more than happy to spend time with him up there.'

'What a glorious thought!' Justin laid his head on the settee. 'I'll have to ask him how he does it.'

'Justin,' Mel warned.

Her brother laughed softly. 'If you could see your face! OK. Is that why you disapprove of him?'

Mel was truly tempted to tell her brother that she had the sneaking suspicion Etienne Hurst had, out of the blue, taken an interest in her along entirely different lines from the fate of his sister's stepchildren, but she stopped herself.

'Uh—no. That has nothing to do with me. He…he's urging me to sell Raspberry Hill, well, not urging exactly but he pointed out today that there may be no other way to go.' She stopped and sighed.

'Oh, hell.' Justin sat up and reached for her hand. 'I'm sorry, Mel. I knew things weren't good but I didn't realise it was that bad. What will we do? I can't imagine losing this place.' He looked around.

Not to mention each other, Mel didn't say, but it was the core problem she always came back to.

'I'm certainly not going to give up without a fight! The accountant will have a clearer picture in a few days—'

'I can always leave school right now,' Justin broke in.

'No! I mean, no, it hasn't come to that yet. And don't pass any of this on to Tosh or Ewan.'

Justin cast her a speaking look. 'What do you think I am? I know, you're still thinking of the rum-rampage, but I've reformed.'

'I wasn't thinking of that at all, but I hope you have!'

He grinned at her, although a touch ashamedly, and presently took himself off to bed, leaving her alone with her thoughts.

She began to tidy up absently, but one thing Justin had said stuck in her mind. It was something she'd never admitted to herself in so many words but there had been a time when Etienne had occupied her dreams. At fifteen, for a while, she'd thought about him rather a lot. However, she'd been so sure she was beneath his notice, it had all died a natural death.

She stopped what she was doing with a tennis racket in one hand and a pair of roller-blades in the other—*or had it*? Perhaps she'd resented being completely beneath his notice and it had been a contributing factor to her so-called dislike of him?

She put the racket in a wooden locker and the roller-blades on a shelf. Not an edifying thought, she conceded. But did that explain the effect he was having on her at the moment?

She couldn't come up with an answer so she took herself to bed, not dreaming that she would have to encounter Etienne Hurst the very next day.

It started out like any other spring day.

Cool, dry and crisp but giving promise of becoming

hot and glorious. Until she noticed a plume of smoke coming from one of the 'resting' paddocks, and raced down to find a bush fire. She called the fire brigade immediately but the difficulty was water; no convenient mains to hook up to, only a small dam a fair way from the fire.

And she worked as frenziedly as any of the firemen to contain it. There were no casual hands working on the property that day to help so she deployed a bag and a shovel with the best of them, resisting Mrs Bedwell's entreaties to leave it to the men, until her bag was taken out of her fingers and she was bodily removed from the area of flames.

'Who...? What?' she spluttered. 'Let me go! If I lose this feed—'

'Shut up, Mel,' Etienne Hurst said. 'You've done enough.'

'I haven't!'

But she was clamped into a strong pair of arms and held there until she subsided, panting, against his chest.

'How did you know about the fire?' she asked hoarsely.

'Mrs Bedwell rang me. She was convinced you were killing yourself.'

'I wasn't.'

'You don't look too good.' He held her away and raised his eyebrows.

'If you think I care how I look—' But before she could finish tears welled in her eyes and brimmed over, making rivulets in the soot on her cheeks.

He pulled her back into his arms. 'I think you're extraordinarily brave. Why don't you have a good cry?'

'I will,' she wept, 'but only because I'm...I don't know what! I never cry,' she added in extreme frustration.

But cry she did for a couple of minutes. Then it occurred to her that she didn't feel like crying any more; she felt, on the contrary, safe and secure and as if she could stay in Etienne Hurst's arms for a lot longer.

She moved her cheek against his shirt and was visited by an extraordinary mental image—rather than being hot, tired and dirty, she pictured herself rising out of a woodland stream in filtered sunlight, naked and with water streaming off her body. Natural enough since she was hot, tired and dirty, she conceded, but how on earth did Etienne get into the picture?

Why was he there, waiting for her at the edge of the pool and taking the slim, satiny length of her into his arms?

'Er—' she blinked rapidly and cleared her throat as she desperately tried to clear her mind, and she looked up at him bemusedly '—th-thank you. How's it going?'

He studied her pink cheeks then glanced over her shoulder. 'It's out. But they'll stay a while to keep an eye on it. What you need is a wash and a drink.'

He picked her up and carried her over to her ute. 'Since we're both dirty this time,' he said to her with his lips quirking, 'we'll use yours.' He set her on her feet.

Mel gasped as she realised that she'd transferred a considerable amount of her dirt to him. There were black streaks on his otherwise pristine white shirt and mud on his moleskins and shoes. 'I'm so sorry!'

'That's OK,' he said easily. 'In you get.'

She climbed in and he drove them up to the house, commenting along the way that she needed to get her suspension and brakes checked.

'What I need,' she said ruefully, 'is a whole new vehicle.'

'There must be other vehicles—what about the cars your father and Margot drove?' he queried.

She hesitated. 'I had to sell them to pay some bills.'

'You should have consulted me first, Mel.'

'To be honest, it didn't cross my mind,' she replied, 'but what could you have done? The bank manager explained to me that, whereas my father had a credit rating, I have none. Oh, he was very kind and concerned and he explained that, while he'd been quite sure Dad would have pulled Raspberry Hill through this reverse, I was a different matter.' She tipped a hand and sighed.

'I see,' he said slowly.

'Not that it's any of your—'

'Any of my business,' he agreed sardonically. 'Don't you think you've worn that one a bit thin, Mel?'

She glanced across at him and for a moment it crossed her mind to tell him that to have someone like him to lean on during these awful times would be like the answer to prayers she'd yet to pray. But the realisation of this came rather like a blow to her solar plexus and she moved restlessly and sighed in relief when the house came in view. Because it offered the hope of refuge from all the conflicting, bewildering emotions—not to mention strange fantasies—she was subject to.

It was not to be. Mrs Bedwell received her with

open arms and immediately began to shepherd her away to get cleaned up.

'A brandy might be appropriate,' Etienne murmured.

'Good thinking, I'll bring you one too,' Mrs Bedwell said over her shoulder as Batman screamed out of the house and took a flying leap into Etienne's arms. 'Glory be, if nothing else you've made a hit with the damn dog!' she added.

'This is becoming a habit,' Mel said as she rejoined Etienne half an hour later. They were on the veranda because, although he'd washed up and scraped the mud off his shoes, his clothes were still dirty.

'Mmm,' he agreed and poured her a brandy from the decanter on a silver tray Mrs Bedwell had provided along with a dish of nuts and olives.

Her hair was still wet and she wore her clean jeans and floral blouse. Her feet were bare and her expression was still somewhat dazed.

Etienne waited until she'd sipped some of the brandy before saying, 'Mel, are there any other unpaid bills?'

'A couple.' She shrugged.

'Why isn't your accountant helping you to deal with them?'

She looked at him over the rim of her glass. 'His bill is one of them.'

He paused for a beat, then, 'I'd like to see them.'

Her gaze clashed with his and she squared her shoulders but he said with soft menace, 'Don't.'

'What?' she uttered crisply.

'Tell me it's none of my business.'

'It isn't,' she insisted.

He looked around, through the French doors to the elegant sitting room that opened onto the front veranda with its beautiful Persian carpet, its antiques and graceful chairs. 'She was my sister,' he said, with the planes and angles of his face suddenly hard.

'She may have been but I don't want any charity.' Mel fortified herself with another sip of brandy and raised her chin.

'You infuriating...' He drew a breath and forced himself to relax. What was it, he wondered at the same time, that attracted him to this often prickly, difficult girl? Other than the obvious, he thought drily, such as a gorgeous figure she seemed to be unaware of, long, shapely legs she persisted in covering up and a lovely face.

Just that, perhaps? Her lack of awareness of her physical attributes? Along with a good splash of cussed independence, of course, he added to himself, and moved restlessly.

'Uh—I wasn't talking about charity,' he said. 'There's a way of dealing with creditors other than selling off the farm, speaking metaphorically. What you need to do is keep in touch, advise them of your difficulties, ask for extensions—and come up with a plan. That's what I could do for you.' He looked at her ironically.

Mel lowered her chin and her shoulders slumped. 'All right. So long as—'

She didn't finish because the look in his eyes told her it would be dangerous in the extreme to do so. 'Thank you,' she said instead with a slight tremor in her voice.

He sat back and finished his drink. 'What are you doing tonight?'

Her eyes widened in surprise. 'Nothing. The usual, I mean. The boys will be home from school soon, so... Why?'

'You don't think it might be an idea to have a break from Raspberry Hill and all its problems?'

'As in?'

'As in dinner at a restaurant, nothing else,' he said laconically.

'Just you and I?'

'Just you and I, Mel. What's wrong with that?'

'Oh, nothing,' she assured him hastily, 'except that I might fall asleep. I—' she put her head back, stretched her neck and moved her head round a couple of times, '—I guess I did more—'

'More fire-fighting than you should have,' he completed for her. 'All right, we'll take a rain check.' He stood up. 'But I'll take the bills home with me.'

'Well,' she temporised, 'I—'

'Now, Mel.'

Despite her stiffness and feeling of exhaustion, she bounced up. 'Do you have any idea how dictatorial you are, Etienne?'

'Yes,' he drawled. 'It's a good way to get things done. I'm not going home without them,' he warned.

She expressed herself colourfully.

He grinned, and added insult to injury by patting her on the head. 'Just get them, kid.'

'No! I refuse to be treated like a kid let alone called one,' she said through her teeth and stood her ground.

'Well,' his eyes glinted, 'there are ways of dealing with stubborn women that you might prefer.' He put one arm around her, bent her back against it and kissed her thoroughly.

When he'd finished, Mel came up for air absolutely

lost for words and unbelievably conscious of a flood of sensations rushing through her right down to the tips of her toes.

Her lips felt bruised; she touched them involuntarily, but although his kiss had been a violation—she'd neither expected it nor asked for it—by some sort of subtle chemistry it had also been fascinating. While she was pressing against him, with his fingers stroking her throat, her skin had felt like silk, her breasts had tightened, and it had suddenly occurred to her that her hips were deliciously curved beneath his hand—something she'd not given much thought to before.

To make matters worse, her woodland-nymph fantasy had come right back to mind...

'Well,' he said with a lurking smile, 'you're right and I was wrong. You certainly don't feel like a child.'

His gaze skimmed down her body then he waited as a tide of colour rushed into her cheeks, but words escaped her. He smiled a strange little smile. 'May I have the bills now?'

Her lips parted and she breathed deeply, but that was a mistake because it brought the whole smoky, wonderful essence of Etienne Hurst to her—as if she wasn't already dizzy with the taste and feel of him—and all he could think of were her bills.

She made an odd sound in her throat, whirled around and disappeared indoors.

But she didn't take the bills out to him. She seconded Mrs Bedwell to do it and took refuge in her bedroom.

Several minutes later Mrs Bedwell knocked on the door and came in. 'He said to say thanks. He said to tell you he'll be back in a couple of days with a plan... What's wrong with you, Mel?'

'Nothing,' Mel replied, although she was sitting on her bed hugging herself.

'You look a bit shook up,' Mrs Bedwell observed slowly. 'You know, there was really no need for you to go fire-fighting like that.'

'There's every need for me to fight certain fires— uh—Mrs B, would you do me a favour?' Mel stopped hugging herself and looked up at her housekeeper.

'Sure.'

But Mel took an exasperated breath because to ask her housekeeper to stop calling on Etienne Hurst and inviting him to lunch could have unforeseen consequences, knowing Mrs Bedwell as she did. 'Nothing.'

'OK.' Mrs Bedwell shrugged. 'What do you mean about ''certain'' fires?'

'It was just a figure of speech, Mrs B.' She got up and tried to collect herself. 'What's for dinner?'

'That's for me to know and you to wonder about!' It was Mrs Bedwell's stock answer and, having delivered it, she bestowed one more curious glance on Mel, and then left her to herself.

CHAPTER FOUR

FOUR days later, Etienne was back.

Four terribly anxious days for Mel, since she'd received advice through her solicitor that, as she had no close relatives, the Department of Family Services would be looking into the situation of her brothers.

This time, she was presiding over coffee and homemade shortbread while trying her best to be composed and as if she'd never been kissed witless by this man.

It was a sparkling day as early spring graced the region, and from the vantage point of Raspberry Hill the waters of the Narrows glinted in the sun and the mock-orange bushes below the veranda were scenting the air.

For some reason she had dressed up for this encounter, well, as much as she ever dressed up, which was to say that she wore a three-quarter flared denim skirt belted into her waist and a fresh white blouse. Her hair was tied back in a white scrunchie.

In contrast, Etienne, in jeans, a khaki bush shirt and short boots, looked much more like a farmer than she did.

He'd greeted her casually and with absolutely no reference to their last encounter. He'd also put a buff folder on the table but made no mention of it, although she couldn't help her eyes being drawn to it frequently.

So they made small talk while they drank their coffee and Batman made his usual fuss of Etienne.

Then she could stand the suspense no longer. 'Have you—' she cleared her throat '—have you come up with a plan, Etienne?'

He drummed his fingers on the folder then he put Batman down and got up to stroll over to the railing and stare out over the view for a couple of minutes.

Finally he turned to her, folded his arms and said, 'I think it would be a good idea if we got married, Mel.'

She stared at him uncomprehendingly. 'Is that the plan?' she said eventually then added stupidly, 'Why me?'

He allowed himself a brief smile and from then on divided his attention between her and the sparkling view. 'Isn't it obvious? Raspberry Hill needs a lot of help, the boys need a father figure, and you yourself could do with a steadying hand to steer you down the right path.'

Sheer rage glinted out of her deep blue eyes. 'How dare you?'

He observed her white face and pinched nostrils with, if anything, a trace of wryness.

'Mel,' he said, 'you obviously have no resources to go on.' He gestured to the folder lying on the table. 'The only way to deal with that is either to declare yourself bankrupt or sell the place.'

'No!'

'Believe me,' he murmured.

She started to feel icy cold. 'But—anyway, I don't see what that's got to do with me needing a steadying hand!'

He shrugged. 'You do have a slightly erratic reputation.'

'What on earth are you talking about?'

'Did you or did you not,' he looked humorous, 'attempt to ride your horse into the Gladstone Council Chambers last year, thereby causing all sorts of chaos, and what about the famous rum party you gave only six months ago?'

'Speaking chronologically,' she replied through her teeth, 'when I found Rimfire he was just a bag of bones. I couldn't *believe* anyone could treat a horse that badly and I didn't see why they shouldn't be prosecuted, but getting the council to agree was another matter. So I decided to take it right to their doorstep.'

'I see. But you not only caused a debacle in the centre of town, you also frightened the life out of the clerk on the door.'

'If she hadn't started screaming, Rimfire wouldn't have spooked. But no one was hurt,' she pointed out.

'There could have been an element of luck in that. How about the party?'

'As I told the magistrate,' she replied with all the hauteur she could muster, 'it got gatecrashed by some hoons. They brought the rum and they caused all the damage.'

'All the same, you're still saddled with not the Boston tea party but the Raspberry Hill rum-rampage tag—and you didn't come away without a warning, Mel.'

'That's because I...' she paused and twined her fingers together '...well, in the confusion I hit a policeman who was mistakenly trying to arrest *me*.'

'I believe you didn't have permission from your father to hold that party, Mel, because he was away at the time and unable to protect you from hoons and gatecrashers.'

She looked briefly uncomfortable. 'I'm nineteen. Quite old enough to hold a party off my own bat, I would have thought. OK! I was wrong, but it could have happened to anyone.'

'They say trouble attracts trouble,' he observed.

'And it could be said,' she responded sweetly, 'that marriage to you sounds like a term at a reform school. No, thank you, Etienne. I appreciate your concern for Raspberry Hill and the boys but we'll manage somehow.'

'What about my concern for you?'

Mel opened her mouth then shut it rather sharply as that cool, alert gaze of his drifted over her. And once again she found herself trapped in his sights, his sole focus, and experiencing the twin sensations of being hunted and quivering inwardly with the memory of his mouth on hers, his hard body against her...

She came out of her reverie with a jolt as he said her name questioningly.

'Uh—what kind of concern is that?'

He smiled. 'I think you have the makings of good wife material.'

She raised her eyebrows imperiously. 'Is that so? Forgive me, but I think you're quite wrong. Mainly because I have no aspirations to be anyone's wife but least of all yours.'

He shrugged. 'Well, that aside, the alternative is to sell off Raspberry Hill and see Justin, Ewan and Tosh go into foster care.'

'No!' She said it quite definitely.

'Just no?'

'Even if I have to sell Raspberry Hill, I'll be able to make a home for them somewhere!'

'Mel, you're still only nineteen; I don't think a court would even consider placing them in your care. And Raspberry Hill is mortgaged to the hilt. There won't be any money to spare.'

'Thanks to your sister,' she shot back.

'Not entirely,' he returned coolly. 'And she may have been my sister but perhaps you should examine your real reason for disliking her as much as you did.'

Mel flinched then opted for honesty with a queer little sigh. 'OK, I was as jealous as hell. We'd had Dad on his own for so long after our mother died then, well, he was besotted with Margot, but the fact remains that—' she looked around with sudden tears in her eyes '—it did all start to go downhill after he married her.'

'You wouldn't have that problem with me.'

Mel wiped her eyes on the back of her hand and stared stonily out to sea as she examined the unpalatable truth of this.

'It's still…' she shook her head in frustration '…it just doesn't make sense. We don't even know each other that well. Look, I'm sorry if I sound ungrateful—most girls would probably jump at the chance but…I guess I'm not most girls,' she finished rather lamely, and stood up.

'And I probably wouldn't be doing this if you were,' he murmured and straightened. 'But I don't believe there's any other way for you to go.' He contemplated her silently.

Mel took an unexpected breath beneath that suddenly authoritative dark glance—it was like running into a brick wall. In a moment, it brought home to her that Etienne Hurst had made up his mind to marry her and would ruthlessly follow it through. Not only that, despite reeling inwardly, she also discovered herself to be in very strange territory on another front.

It was the most amazing sensation. One part of her was outraged to think he believed he could offer her marriage out of the blue and that she would keel over immediately and accept. While the other half was undoubtedly impressed not only by his authority and power but also by him as a man.

What qualities about him, she wondered, were capable of causing her to fantasise about him at the same time as she hated his arrogance?

She wasn't left to wonder for long. He strolled over to her and put his hands on her shoulders. 'Think about it, Miss Ethridge, but in the meantime perhaps this will help you to see the light.'

He kissed her again, not deeply this time, but lingeringly and quite sufficiently for one of those qualities in him she'd pondered so recently to leap out at her—raw sex appeal.

In fact, everything about him appealed to her in those moments and the feel of his lean, hard body drew a primitive response from her own body. A yearning to be captured by him and brought gloriously alive in the most intimate way, so much so—and so much did it take her by surprise—she gasped beneath his mouth and shuddered beneath his hands.

He lifted his head and looked into her wide, stunned eyes with the faintest smile twisting his lips.

'I'll be back,' he said, and she wasn't sure whether it was a threat or a promise.

Whatever it was, it kept her rooted to the spot while he strode down the steps towards his car. How long she would have been paralysed like that she was not to know if it hadn't been for Mrs Bedwell.

With her trademark stalk, reminiscent of a tall, thin bird, Mrs Bedwell came round the corner of the house to waylay Etienne just before he got to his car.

Having had Mrs Bedwell meddle in her life for as long as she could remember, Mel came out of her reverie and slipped discreetly inside. She sprinted down the hall towards the study, from where she would be closest to the drive.

So that, lurking beneath the study window, she heard Mrs Bedwell say to Etienne, 'Mr Hurst, I think that's a very good idea of yours.'

'You do?' came Etienne's reply. 'What idea is that?'

'The idea of marrying Mel. I've been going crazy trying to work out what's to become of them since their father died. And your sister,' she added conscientiously.

There was silence and Mel peeped over the study window sill to see Etienne stopped in his tracks by Mrs Bedwell's eavesdropping habits.

Which Mrs Bedwell took full advantage of to continue volubly, 'You see, I always did reckon Mel was born one gene short. For that matter, Justin is turning out the same, and as for Tosh...' Mrs Bedwell threw up her hands and shook her head.

'I don't think I quite understand,' Etienne murmured, as Mel's mouth dropped open in disbelief.

'They never stop to think, *that* gene,' Mrs Bedwell elucidated. 'Got it from their mother, they did. With all the best intentions in the world she was never out of trouble! I told Mel people wouldn't take kindly to her taking her horse to the council, I told her not to hold that party—believe me, there's a million things I've told her not to do, but once she gets a bee in her bonnet there's no stopping her. Where will she end, I keep wondering, without someone strong like you?'

'I…see,' Etienne replied cautiously.

'Then,' Mrs Bedwell placed her hand on Etienne's arm and stared confidingly into his eyes, 'there's the way she's grown up. Who would have thought such a skinny tomboy with those awful braces on her teeth and forever scratched and grazed would grow into such a looker?'

Mel ducked her head, grimaced, and awaited Etienne's reply with bated breath. But he didn't reply and Mrs Bedwell went on.

'Not that she knows it. You can accuse her of a lot of things but vanity isn't one of them. Problem is— there are a lot of unscrupulous men out there and once they find out that all they need is some kind of crazy *cause* to worm their way into her heart, who knows what could happen?'

'Mrs Bedwell, I could *strangle* you,' Mel said through her teeth. Unfortunately, this caused her to miss what Mrs Bedwell said next and consequently she had no idea what it was that prompted Etienne to reply that he had become increasingly aware of it and would certainly take it into consideration.

'*What?*' Mel muttered, severely frustrated.

But Mrs Bedwell only said then, 'Good, well, I can leave it up to you?'

'You may, Mrs Bedwell,' he answered as he shook her hand then got into his car and drove off.

It was not in Mel's nature to bottle things up so she accosted Mrs Bedwell immediately and asked her what she thought she was doing by encouraging a man they barely knew to marry her.

A short, sharp argument ensued on who had the right to eavesdrop *when*. Then Mrs Bedwell announced that it so happened her nephew worked for Etienne Hurst so she knew quite a lot about him and all of it good. She also added pithily that if Mel hadn't so resolutely distanced herself from her stepmama, she'd know a lot more about the man herself.

'He's made a fortune with his own hands,' she stated. 'He's an excellent employer, a darn good businessman and he's very highly thought of in the community.'

'He may be,' Mel shot back, 'but he's also extremely arrogant, and what's that got to do with me marrying him? There's no love lost between us, I can assure you!'

'Love!' Mrs Bedwell echoed with consummate scorn. 'I married Jack Bedwell for love and five years later he walked out on me never to be seen again, leaving me with three kids to rear on my own. Love,' she repeated bitterly; 'what good did it do me? Here I am not even in my own home and a slave to a family that's half-mad!'

They were in the kitchen during this exchange, and Mel suddenly changed tack.

'Sit down, Mrs B,' she ordered. She poured her a

cup of coffee and took it along with some shortbread over to her.

Then she sank on her knees in front of her and said softly, 'You do know this whole place would fall apart without you, don't you?'

Mrs Bedwell pursed her lips.

'You do know,' Mel continued, 'that we love you and consider you part of the family and we'd be devastated if you left and went to the Calders up the road who are always trying to pinch you from us?'

Mrs Bedwell's face softened.

'And who,' Mel smiled up at her with a teasing glint in her eyes, 'is the real authority in this house?'

Mrs Bedwell sighed then smiled herself. 'You're a sweetie, Mel. Just promise me one thing—you think seriously about Etienne Hurst. Because I know you well enough to know that losing the boys and Raspberry Hill on top of losing your dad would nearly kill you.'

So Mel thought about it until she could have screamed.

So many pros, she had to marvel. Just take the boys. There was no doubting Justin could be a handful at times, and what no one knew, because she'd chosen not to reveal it, was that he had been responsible for the notorious Raspberry Hill rum-rampage.

He'd got in with a dubious crowd of older boys whom he'd invited to the party with such disastrous results. She was pretty sure the fact that she'd had to front a magistrate had brought home the error of his ways to him. But she couldn't deny that he might need a strong hand to steer him through his late teens.

Then there was Ewan. Thin and dark, at twelve, he was a chronic asthmatic with little interest in school and whose sole ambition in life was to paint. And Tosh, who had no redeeming chestnut in his hair—it was plain ginger—and if someone up there had set out to create another *Just William*, they'd succeeded in Tosh.

Her father's favourite saying about his youngest child had been that he got into more trouble than Flash Gordon.

All the same, she loved them all desperately and couldn't even begin to think about losing them.

So why do the cons seem to be overwhelming when there are so many pros? she asked herself as she tossed and turned one night.

Don't be thick, Mel, she answered herself, using Mrs Bedwell's favourite put-down. This is a marriage of convenience you're being offered, that's why it's sticking in your throat! He may have kissed you and he may look at you as if he'd like to sweep you onto his charger and make off with you whether you like it or not, but his reputation is *not* consistent with Etienne Hurst suddenly falling in *love* with a girl like you...

She punched her pillow and tried to get more comfortable. It *was* well-known in the Gladstone area that for his recreation he'd leased and renovated an abandoned lighthouse keeper's house on top of a craggy headland and that he spent some of his free time there, fishing and crabbing the waters of a protected lagoon at the base of the headland.

It was rumoured that there was no more fulfilling an experience for a woman than to be bedded by

Etienne Hurst in his lighthouse eyrie then treated to a seafood banquet. It appeared to be a fact that there were plenty of willing women but—here lay the rub—mature, sophisticated, glamorous women who were a very far cry from nineteen-year-old Melinda Ethridge, whom, no one could deny, he often treated like an exasperating kid.

So, what did he really want from her? Was it only out of a sense of responsibility towards his sister's stepchildren that he'd proposed marriage? Surely not. But then, despite sounding and acting like the quintessential Australian, had his French mother instilled old-fashioned notions about arranged marriages in him?

Even if that was so, she reasoned, what had she to contribute to an arranged marriage? As far as she could see, all she would bring with her was a sea of debt and three sometimes-difficult boys.

Of course, Raspberry Hill was a very desirable property. With an injection of funds it could more than pay its way but Etienne could probably buy six Raspberry Hills, so...

'It just doesn't make sense,' she told herself yet again. 'Unless he does want me in a purely physical way for the time being, does he feel a sense of responsibility for us? And at the same time he's decided he can mould me into a suitable wife for the long-term business of providing him with heirs whilst he continues his lifestyle much as he always has?'

She sat up suddenly, feeling cold and a little sick. In the absence of any declarations of love, and how could there be, what else was she to think? On the subject of being moulded into a suitable wife for a man she barely knew, she had plenty to think about and chief amongst her thoughts was the one that scared her to death.

Yes, she may have been bowled over a bit by Etienne once, but *this* really opened up a yawning chasm at her feet. The chasm of man-woman relationships, a subject she'd reached the grand old age of nineteen without giving much thought to at all.

One reason for this was that, being horse, dog, country and farming mad all her life and possessing three brothers, she'd always been 'one of the boys'.

And she had been a late developer—Mrs Bedwell was right. No one, and least of all herself, had foreseen that she would ever be other than skinny, active and far more interested in boyish pursuits and all the causes she felt so passionately about, rather than clothes, her appearance and boys for their own sake.

So it had to have come as a shock to find Etienne Hurst suddenly trapping her in his sights. Nor could she any longer continue in confusion over his intentions. What he'd proposed may have 'convenience' and 'arranged' written all over it but it certainly wouldn't be a marriage in name only. She may have been a late developer but she wasn't that naïve, and certainly not since she'd really thought it through and been so effectively kissed...

She stopped battling with her bedclothes and got up to cross over to the window to see that dawn was rimming the horizon. And finally she allowed her mind to dwell not on pros and cons as such but the sensations he aroused in her. The sort of dangerous delight he brought to her when he touched her and kissed her.

She took a quick breath as she thought of the strength of his arms, the sprinkling of black hairs on them and the powerful width of his shoulders. But, at the same time as she felt a rippling of desire run through her just to think of those things, she still had the strange conviction she was playing with fire…

CHAPTER FIVE

WHEN Melinda Ethridge agreed to marry Etienne Hurst, she made the conscious decision to be an unconventional bride. Not that she mentioned it other than obliquely when she summoned him to Raspberry Hill to discuss his proposal.

This time she received him in the formal lounge, surrounded by all the evidence of his sister's exquisite but expensive taste.

She cleared her throat twice as she stood in front of him. 'Etienne—oh, please do sit down!'

'Thank you,' he murmured but waited until she'd sat down, straight-backed and on the edge of a gilt-framed, spindly chair before choosing a more substantial one for himself.

'Etienne,' she began again with her hands clasped in the lap of the denim skirt she wore again with her white blouse, 'thank you for your offer of marriage. I'm thinking about accepting it.'

'Are you, Mel?' His lips quirked.

She suffered a moment of nervous dread that he'd changed his mind and she was making a fool of herself then a spark of wrath lit her eyes. 'Are you laughing at me? If so, would you like to share the joke?'

He observed her tense, upright posture and the lines of strain in her face. 'It struck me that you could well have been thinking about lining up in front of a firing squad, Mel, that's all,' he replied gravely.

She breathed exasperatedly. 'Of course I'm not but this isn't easy!'

'Why not?'

She controlled an urge to throw one of his sister's beautiful Chinese porcelain bowls at him. 'Take my word for it, it is not, Etienne,' she said in a chilly way and shrugged. 'Perhaps women are different but…well, how to agree to a marriage of convenience in order to save your home and your family doesn't feature in the etiquette books!'

'Probably not.' He looked amused.

'Nor is it easy to know what kind of emotions one should be experiencing,' she continued.

'One could remind oneself that one has been happy to be kissed on occasion, very happy,' he contributed.

She regarded him witheringly. 'If that's all there is to it, all I can say is, you must be incredibly naïve.'

He laughed aloud this time. 'Maybe one of us is— I'm not sure which one.'

But Mel refused to be amused or sidetracked. 'Etienne, I may be only nineteen but I'm not that naïve and I'm not stupid—'

She broke off as a piteous whine came from the doorway into the hall. She turned to see Batman sitting in the doorway literally quivering with the injustice of being expressly forbidden to enter the lounge so he couldn't get to Etienne.

'Good heavens!' She looked at the dog in astonishment. 'That's the only rule he's ever obeyed!'

'He's not allowed in here?'

'He is not!' Mel shuddered.

'Then maybe we could take this—conference outside. I must admit,' Etienne glanced around, 'the formality of this room on top of your formality is a little daunting.'

Mel swallowed a pithy retort. 'Oh, all right. We could take a walk in the garden.'

Batman was ecstatic. He jumped straight into Etienne's arms as soon as he crossed out of the lounge. 'My one fan,' Etienne murmured with a decidedly wicked look at Mel.

'He doesn't have to marry you,' she replied.

'True. So. You were saying, Mel?'

But she waited until they were strolling across the lawn towards the edge of the headland before she spoke again, this time with quiet determination.

'In a nutshell, being neither particularly naïve nor stupid, Etienne, I need to know what I'm letting myself in for.'

Batman was on the ground by this time, scurrying about investigating delicious scents and intoxicating trails.

'Do you mean, what kind of a wife I have in mind for you to be?'

She blinked. 'Yes. As well as what kind of a husband *you* intend to be.'

'Oh, the usual.'

'What is that?' she asked frostily.

'Well,' he stopped as they came to a fence and propped a foot on the bottom bar, 'the kind that prefers to be with his mates at the pub or the footy for the most part.'

She eyed him incredulously.

'As for my wife,' he continued, 'I'd expect a good cook, although we do have Mrs Bedwell so we could cross that off the list. Uh—good with kids, naturally, and appreciative that her place is very definitely in the home changing nappies, but at the same time able to mow the lawn…as a matter of fact, Mel, you come highly recommended in that area; I wouldn't have to lift a finger—'

'Stop!' she commanded. 'I'm serious!' But in fact, much against her will but all the same, she was laughing. 'You're crazy!'

'No.' He reached for her hand. 'But I'm glad you've got a sense of humour.'

She sobered. 'Did you doubt it?'

He looked down at her. 'Perhaps we haven't had much to laugh about lately. Look, I'm perfectly happy for you just to be yourself.'

'What about—us not being in love?'

'Maybe we can make it happen.'

'And if we don't?'

'Time will tell.'

A little chill ran through her.

'But what—' she looked frustrated '—say we'd got married and you'd discovered I didn't have a sense of humour?'

He looked out over the view in silence for a long moment then down at her hand in his. 'Mel, you may not know this but the first time I saw you in over a year, I wanted you immediately.'

She stared at him wide-eyed and with her lips parted.

'It's not so inconceivable, you know.' His lips twisted. 'It happens. Didn't you guess?'

'I...I...thought I must be imagining it,' she said huskily.

'No. Nor has it changed or gone away. I don't usually,' he said with irony, 'go about kissing girls I don't like.'

Mel tried desperately to sort through the new emotions this aroused in her. Much as she couldn't deny that Etienne Hurst fascinated her, neither could she, once again, stifle a little feeling of fear at the same time. To do, she discovered, with the uncertainty of whether she could ever match this worldly, experienced man...

'So...so—'

'So, we have a good basis for putting together a marriage. You need me. I need you.'

But for how long will you need me? The question was on the tip of her tongue but in the end she was unable to utter it.

'Will...will I be able to go on as I have been?' she asked instead.

'More or less.' He grinned suddenly. 'I guess we'll both have to make a few adjustments to our lifestyles but if you're happy to go on being taken up with Raspberry Hill, that's fine.'

'I don't suppose you'll have much time for it?' she said tentatively.

'We'll see. Can I ask you a question?'

She nodded after a moment.

He turned around and leant back against the fence.

He wore his blue short-sleeved shirt today with khaki trousers and boots. 'How do you feel about me?'

'The million-dollar question,' she said quizzically, and received an appreciative glance in return. 'The thing is,' she sighed suddenly, 'I don't know.'

'I don't mean,' he said slowly, 'are-you-prepared-to-go-to-the-ends-of-the-earth-and-back-for-me kind of thing. But might you,' he paused and turned sideways so he could watch her, 'might you have got over the supreme suspicion and distaste you—apparently—used to feel?'

She lowered her lashes. 'Yes. I might.'

'Well, that's a start.' There was a slightly dry note in his voice and her lashes flew up but he was staring at her enigmatically.

'Then how long do you think it will be before you're able to make up your mind?' he queried.

That was when stark reality hit Mel. What choice did she have? It was either do this, or face losing the boys... 'I have made up my mind,' she said quietly. 'I'll do it.'

'Mel,' he took her chin in his hands, and shook his head, 'you—'

'No, I've decided to go ahead—I don't have much choice and it was either say yes now and get it over and done with, or go on agonising about it all and I'm tired of that!'

'But you're still going to hold it against me?' he said softly, with something she couldn't identify in his expression.

'Not at all,' she denied. 'Well, as far as I can tell at this stage, no. Just one thing—I would rather we didn't carry on like two lovebirds before the deed is done. I wouldn't feel too comfortable about that.'

'And after the deed is done?' He raised an ironic eyebrow.

'Time will tell, Etienne.'

For a moment she thought she'd really surprised him as his eyes narrowed. Then he surprised her. 'Yes, ma'am. I'm thoroughly on my mettle now and will undertake to behave myself in the interim. After I've done this, that is.'

For a moment he trailed his fingers down her cheek then he bent his head to kiss her very lightly.

Mel stirred beneath his mouth as all her senses were invaded, and the promise of delicious rapture would have been, so tantalisingly, within her grasp had she not denied it to herself with her own strictures.

He drew away.

Her lips quivered and the tendrils of coppery hair framing her face danced in the light breeze while her velvety blue eyes were slightly desolate, and her breasts beneath the thin cotton blouse moved up and down in tune with her ragged breathing.

'You did say—' he began, with his dark eyes focused squarely on what her breathing was doing to the front of her blouse.

'I know what I said,' she whispered then took hold of her disappointment and tried, resolutely, to banish it.

After all, she thought, it might not be a bad idea to retain some will-power before she married Etienne Hurst, since she really did not know exactly what she felt about him. And it might be a good idea not to allow him to feel he had too much of an upper hand over her because, while she might have no choice but to marry him, she fully intended to retain some independence.

She squared her shoulders—and detected a glint of something unfathomable in his gaze as he raised his eyes suddenly to hers. Could it be self-directed mockery? she wondered briefly and surprisingly. Then it was gone and she pursued her line of thought—this was undoubtedly an unconventional marriage, so why shouldn't she be an unconventional bride-to-be?

'I did mean it,' she said.

'So—' he paused for a beat '—so be it.'

'How…when will we do it?'

He folded his arms. 'I don't see much point in dragging it out, do you?'

'No…' she said slowly, and felt herself grow hot beneath his quizzical regard.

'As soon as it can be arranged, then?'

Batman pelted up and deposited a very old tennis ball at their feet then grinned hugely up at them.

Etienne retrieved the ball and lobbed it away.

'All right,' she agreed, 'but let's also make it as simple as possible.'

He wiped his hands on his trousers. 'You could always leave it up to me.'

'That would certainly be—unconventional,' she murmured, but when he looked at her narrowly she shrugged. 'If you wouldn't mind?'

'Not at all. So long as we have a deal, Mel?'

She put out her hand. 'We have a deal.'

He took her hand but she could see his amusement and for a moment she was terribly tempted to do something essentially out of character such as—oh, no, she thought, not another fantasy! She closed her eyes tight.

Her mind's eye resisted all her attempts to smother it, however, and she pictured herself dressed in a filmy, silvery, flowing gown, floating over the grass, not with a Jack Russel puppy but a cheetah cub in a jewelled collar, towards Etienne. And taking his hand and pulling him down into the grass where she then proceeded to unbutton his shirt and run her hands along his shoulders and tantalise him with her lips and her body until he begged for more...

'Mel?'

Her eyes flew open to see him looking down at her curiously. She went hot and cold with embarrassment and wondered wildly where these strange images came from—*cheetah cubs*? Or was this fantasy a representation of how she dearly wished she could be—sure of herself, sure of her powers of attraction for him, different, devastating—?

He said her name again.

'Uh...I was saying,' she frowned in awful concentration as she tried to remember what on earth she had been saying, 'that...we have a deal, that's all.'

'Sure?'

'Quite sure. I don't change my mind once I've given my word.' She tried to sound as airy as possible but she could see that he was still curious.

Fortunately Batman saved her by running up with

his ball again, and this time it was she who threw it for him with all her might.

A couple of weeks later, very early on the morning of her wedding day, she examined that decision to be unconventional and decided that, despite Etienne's insistence on a church wedding, she'd held pretty well to her resolve.

The sun was rising over Raspberry Hill as she sat in a cane rocker on the veranda in her Snoopy pyjamas with a cup of tea and thought back over the last weeks that had simply flown from the day she'd agreed to Etienne's proposal.

There had been moments when she'd regretted the conditions she'd laid down for the run-up to the wedding or, perhaps, regretted the sense of hostility and tension within her that had prompted her to impose them. But nothing could change the fact that her feelings on the subject of Etienne Hurst were most ambiguous, just as her feelings about having to marry him to save her home and her family were difficult to deal with.

But when she saw the ease with which he got on with the boys, when he outlined the plans he had for Raspberry Hill, she did sometimes wonder whether she shouldn't have simply buried her antagonism towards being married to a man who wanted her but didn't love her, and gone with the flow? Even thrown herself into the wedding preparations rather than preserving a rather prickly distance from it all?

As for the boys, both Ewan and Tosh had accepted the idea of their sister marrying Etienne on its face value, but Justin had divined the true state of affairs and had lined himself up solidly on Mrs Bedwell's side of the fence. Although he had said to Mel that, if Etienne made her skin crawl, not even to give his proposal a second thought, and they would find some other way of managing. .

The irony of that was that no one really believed Etienne could make any woman's skin crawl but it was an irony that irked Mel considerably.

Even if he didn't make her skin crawl, however, what he did do to her was no open book. She might get trapped into the odd fantasy about him, but since the day she'd agreed to marry him Etienne had been most circumspect, as requested. In fact, if it hadn't been for a couple more of those hunter-still looks she'd encountered when she'd least expected it, she'd have thought herself safe, although that posed a question... Why would someone who experienced rather vividly intimate fantasies about a man feel safe when he ignored her?

Of course, today would change all that; she'd be foolish to pretend otherwise to herself.

She stirred, pleated her pyjama leg and stared out over the garden. There was a frilly lizard sunning itself on a rock, and two kookaburras sitting immobile and quite silent in a gum tree, watching it intently. Then she became aware that she was no longer the only one up.

She sniffed the air and the delicious aroma of frying bacon told her that Mrs Bedwell was out and about. A couple of thumps echoed from Justin's bedroom—his latest hobby was weightlifting—and she could hear Tosh talking to Batman.

No sound of Ewan; was he all right? she wondered as she always wondered. Then he she heard him bitterly telling Tosh his damn dog had chewed one of his socks, and she relaxed.

But she knew suddenly she could never get through this day without doing two things, and without bothering to change or put on shoes she ran down the steps and through the damp grass to her father's favourite spot on all of Raspberry Hill.

It was a spot on the headland, where many years ago he had built her a swing. And from where, when she was a little girl, he'd pointed out the Narrows, the strip of water that separated Curtis Island from the mainland. What was unusual about the Narrows was that at low tide it was high and dry and used as a cattle crossing to bring stock across from the island, whereas at high tide small ships could sail over the fences.

The swing was still there, although she could barely fit onto it now, but she wedged herself in and caressed the frayed ropes as she thought of her father with deep, deep sorrow. But at least he would know, surely he would know, she thought, that in his place she was taking care of the family. For that matter, she recalled, he'd always got on well with Etienne Hurst...

She watched as a trawler, with its nets tucked up like a woman holding up her skirts, steamed towards Ramsay's Crossing. Then she closed her eyes, swallowed several times, and went to see her horse.

Rimfire, a chestnut gelding, heard her coming and his lovely long face with its white blaze and pricked ears was turned towards her over the half-door of the stable as he whickered excitedly.

She flung her arms round his neck to receive his familiar nuzzle of her shoulder before hunger got the better of him and he nipped her gently.

'OK. OK! I know, I may be getting married today, believe it or not, but first things first,' she crooned. And not only did she mix his feed but she also cleaned out his stall and brushed him until he shone.

'Now, I'm going away for a week,' she told him, 'but Justin has sworn to look after you, so don't pine, don't sulk and don't you dare kick him or bite him! I know you don't like men but all the same—'

'*Melinda!*'

She turned to see Mrs Bedwell bearing down on her.

'I'm coming, I'm coming, Mrs B!'

'Mel, it's your wedding day! You shouldn't be cleaning out horse stalls—what am I going to do with you?'

Mel kissed Rimfire on his velvety nose, took a deep breath and turned to Mrs Bedwell. 'OK—what did you have in mind?'

'A bath, your hair—oh, look at your nails! I—'

But Mel put an arm around Mrs Bedwell. 'I'm all yours,' she said gravely.

Three hours later she was ready, as unconventionally ready to be a bride as she knew how.

In the first instance, no one was giving her away.

In the second, she had no bridesmaids; rather, her three brothers were not so much attendants but guardians of honour. Then there was her outfit, hardly a traditional bridal gown.

Made of a soft, shimmering fabric, it wasn't white but pale blue and it wasn't a dress but a top and a three-quarter skirt with a definite gypsy flavour. The top was gathered and shirred around the shoulders with short puff sleeves. The skirt had a flounce around the bottom and she wore a topaz sash around her waist. The topaz colour was repeated in a choker necklace of six strands of glass beads and gilt bars around her slender neck and she wore dangly gilt and diamanté earrings set with seed-pearls.

She would have carried no flowers if Mrs Bedwell hadn't, with tears in her eyes, insisted she couldn't get married without a bouquet and a garter to throw, but she'd won the battle to wear no veil and her chestnut hair was simply tied back with a flower and long, wavy tendrils framing her face.

'Wow!'

'Blimey!'

'Holy moly!'

Justin, Tosh and Ewan all looked stunned by her appearance as she stepped into the lounge, where they were assembled waiting for her.

'Does that mean—what does that mean?' she asked with a grin.

'As the oldest brother,' Justin quelled the other two with a glance, 'may I say you look simply sensational, Mel?'

'I don't see why you should be the only spokesman, Justin, you look just lovely, Mel,' Ewan contributed.

'Well, you sure look like a girl,' Tosh commented. 'Mel, Mellie, please can I take Batman with us to the wedding? He'll be so lonely!'

'No!' It was such a chorus, even Tosh, who rarely took no for an answer, shrugged and desisted. And together—Mrs Bedwell, looking regal in purple with a pink flower-garden hat had left a few minutes earlier with her nephew—they made their way to the waiting limousine.

On the face of it, it was a glorious day for a wedding. The clear blue skies of early spring presided over the dark green folds of Mount Larcom, whose craggy peak, in turn, presided over Gladstone, Curtis Island and the waters of the Narrows, shimmering in the sunlight.

'Mel?'

She turned to Justin.

'Only about ten minutes to go until we get to the church. How do you feel, sis?'

'Nervous, I guess.' She twined her fingers together.

'Why?' Tosh queried.

'You wouldn't understand,' Justin replied loftily.

'It's a big step, getting married,' Ewan explained with more patience.

'Why? It feels like a party to me!' Tosh patted his new suit, his first, with palpable pride.

'It's probably harder for girls,' Ewan said reflectively. 'They've got to worry about how they look and all that. But at least you're luckier than most girls, Mel. You don't have to change homes.'

And therein lies the kernel, Mel thought as she stared out of the window.

'Mel?'

It was Justin again, as the limousine slowed and turned into the churchyard.

She withdrew her gaze from the old wooden church with its small white bell tower. 'Yes?'

'He's a good bloke—and you've still got us. Always. Hasn't she, boys?'

Ewan and Tosh agreed fervently.

Mel stared into Justin's blue eye, so like her own, then smiled shakily. 'Thanks.' And they all leaned forward and crossed hands as they'd always done in moments of unity.

Seconds later the limousine pulled up in front of the church and, taking a deep breath, Mel alighted and went to her wedding.

CHAPTER SIX

THE church was surprisingly full for the small wedding planned.

Mel looked down the aisle and at the populated pews on either side as she hesitated on the porch. She'd agreed to Etienne's suggestion that they get in a wedding consultant to plan the reception he'd also insisted they hold. She now realised that, without his consulting *her*, a larger wedding was about to take place.

It flashed through her mind that it could be her own fault she was unprepared for this. She'd virtually given the consultant carte blanche because she'd found herself unable to be enthusiastic about a wedding that had to be a farce.

Now she regretted that frame of mind as the consultant, a stylish woman of about fifty, came out onto the porch to greet her, at the same time unable to mask a glint of surprise in her eyes.

'Who are all these people?' Mel whispered.

The consultant, Mary Lees, blinked. 'Well, Etienne gave me a guest list... Melinda, I must say you look gorgeous! I knew you wanted to surprise us but you've done so beautifully. It's so unusual but—just you!'

'Thank you,' Mel said distractedly, as Mary smoothed out her skirt and turned her around so she could check the back of it.

'There, perfect,' Mary murmured and turned her attention to the boys. 'My, my!' she enthused. 'Don't you three look gorgeous too? Now, you know what to do? Once your sister reaches the altar, the three of you move into the first pew on the left. Mrs Bedwell is there. Are we ready?' she asked warmly.

Mel swallowed then nodded, and at a signal from Mary Lees the organ swelled and the 'Wedding March' began.

It was the longest walk of Mel's life. She didn't hear the rustle of approbation that rose as she moved down the aisle; she didn't notice the lovely flowers; even the music faded as she concentrated on the tall, dark figure waiting for her in front of the altar.

Then, about three-quarters of the way down the aisle, he turned and their gazes clashed. Like the consultant, a glint of surprise lit his eyes as he took in her shimmering pale blue outfit and one dark eyebrow lifted briefly. And he smiled at her, a smile full of humour and wry understanding that amply signified he knew just what kind of a statement she was making in her blue dress—a protest because this marriage did not have her approval.

To make matters worse, to tell her she'd failed in her protest, as she arrived at his side, he put his hand on her arm and murmured, 'You leave all other brides I've seen for dead, Mel.'

She bit her lip and, thankfully but with considerable irony, surrendered herself to the rituals of the ceremony.

'You may kiss the bride...'

She heard the words in an almost trance-like state,

stared down for a long moment at the ring on her left hand then turned to Etienne Hurst for his kiss.

That was when she saw it again, that so still, so alert dark gaze focused squarely on her, and she shivered visibly as he bent his head and claimed her lips. But he surprised her. Although to all intents and purposes he was kissing her lightly, with his hands now on her waist, he was in fact saying barely audibly against the corner of her mouth.

'Whatever else I may be, Mel, I do have your best interests at heart, so—could we lighten up a bit?'

A ripple of indignation ran through her along with a sense of pride. Was he suggesting that she looked like a martyr? Well, that was the last stance she intended to take and she would show Etienne Hurst she was made of sterner stuff if it killed her!

So instead of being stiff and unyielding in his arms, she forced herself to relax. She also closed her eyes and murmured back, 'OK, I'm ready.'

She felt the jolt of laughter in him and her lashes fluttered up. 'What's wrong?'

'Nothing.'

'Then why aren't you kissing me?'

'I am—now.' His lips closed on hers and his hands moved on her waist and, for one horrified moment, she thought some outlandish scenario along the lines of nude nymphs was going to overtake her.

Not *here*, she commanded herself, and relaxed again, in relief, as her mind remained blank.

All the same, the church receded, all the difficulties of this marriage faded to be replaced by a supreme awareness of Etienne Hurst and—surely not?—surely yes, the conviction that she'd missed being kissed by him.

Then he stopped kissing her and looked into her eyes. And he said to the little flare of shock in them, 'Hello, Mrs Hurst.'

She couldn't think of anything to say but there was no need as he turned her towards the congregation and everyone rose in a delighted wave down the church. Mrs Bedwell burst into tears and rushed out to hug her. Justin, Tosh and Ewan did the same and, for some reason, as the organ swelled again for the triumphal march down the aisle, Mel felt as if she'd achieved something although she wasn't sure what.

And once out on the porch they were strewn with rose petals and confetti, at the centre of a happy crowd of people Mel mostly didn't know but people who loved a wedding obviously—or were happy for Etienne Hurst.

'Not so bad after all,' Etienne said in the limousine as it drew away from the church.

Mel leant forward to wave to the throng. 'Who are all those people?'

'Friends, business acquaintances, people who work for me. You certainly wowed them all!'

Well, I certainly surprised myself, she thought but said instead, trying for a casual approach when in reality she could still feel his hands on her body, 'I must be getting the hang of this wedding business.' She sat back and brushed some rose petals off her top.

'I hope that doesn't mean you intend to make a habit of it?' he returned wryly.

'Not at all. But I wasn't sure if I could handle it. Now I think I can get through the reception with—panache.'

'Good.' But he was laughing.

'What's so funny about that?'

'Your choice of words. I'm not sure I could handle a Mel Ethridge full of panache.'

Mel considered a reply, then a thought struck her. 'They all seemed to be very happy for you, I mean really happy.'

'Could be I'm not such a bad bloke after all.'

Mel chose her words with care. 'It's not that I thought you were bad.'

He glinted her an ironic look. 'Just tarred with the same brush as my sister?' he suggested.

She placed her bouquet on the seat between them and pleated her skirt absently. 'I don't feel really good about myself in regard to Margot. And I apologise for tarring you with the same brush but—'

'You're still not sure about marrying me?'

She bestowed a deep blue, enigmatic gaze on him.

'What?' he queried ruefully. 'You're making me nervous, Mel.'

'What do you expect, Etienne? I may have enjoyed kissing you but that's a far cry from—' she hesitated '—from…'

'Laying down all your arms?' he suggested.

'I would like to know…' She stopped and cleared her throat. 'I would like to know if I'm expected to go to bed with you tonight. I mean, I know, and accept, that it has to happen some time but—' She stopped again.

'I shouldn't take it as an indication that you're

ready to leap into bed with me?' He reached over to take her hand and fiddled with his wedding ring. 'Am I correct in assuming you're a virgin, Mel?'

Some colour rose to her cheeks but she answered honestly, 'Very much so, Etienne. Well, I guess you are or you aren't, just as you can't be a little pregnant, but I don't seem to have had much time for that kind of thing. Either that or I was born another gene short!' She broke off and bit her lip.

She saw the frown in his eyes, then the recognition, then the laughter. 'Do you always eavesdrop on each other?'

'Mrs Bedwell has it down to a fine art and sometimes you have to retaliate in self-defence,' she told him, 'as you will probably discover for yourself. By the way, I do stop to think, frequently!'

'Having seen the agony you've gone through this last month, I believe you,' he said a shade drily.

'Etienne,' it was her turn to frown, 'can you blame me? I would have thought it was a plus that I didn't leap at your offer.'

'Oh, it was,' he drawled. 'But now the deed is done, it would please me and help *you* if you relinquished the burden and left it up to me. You've fought the good fight, Mel.'

She shrugged then replied candidly, 'I don't see what else I can do but just two things. I don't compromise easily. And I don't feel that I can live in a cloud of eternal gratitude to you.'

'Good,' he said again. 'I wouldn't enjoy that at all.'

She stared at him narrowly, thinking that he looked rather wonderful in his dark suit then had to wrest her thoughts away... 'So, about tonight?'

'I'm of the opinion we should take it as it comes,' he said.

With that she had to be content, as the limousine drew up in front of the garden restaurant where the reception was to be held.

Three hours later, Mel left her wedding reception wearing a rather lovely lime linen trouser. Mrs Bedwell had insisted on it and helped her to choose it as well as new silk underwear to wear beneath it, Mel's only concession to a trousseau. She'd changed in the suite provided by the restaurant with Mrs Bedwell's help, after throwing her garter and bouquet. A stranger had caught her garter but a schoolfriend had caught her bouquet.

In truth, though, she'd enjoyed her wedding reception. So had everyone else—perhaps it had been contagious? Along with the delicious food, the best champagne and a lively band? Not that she'd eaten or drunk much at all but she did love to dance and Etienne had proved a good partner. Also, her brothers had enjoyed every minute of it although she suspected even Tosh was a little tipsy.

Now she stood on the pavement beside a sleek, very new-looking sapphire sports car coupé, obviously Etienne's, although she'd never seen it before, with her next test looming, their honeymoon.

She'd made one proviso regarding a honeymoon. She would not consider his lighthouse retreat for the week he'd decided to take off, she'd told him.

'Why not?'

'Too many associations with other women,' she'd replied crisply.

He hadn't looked chastened, he'd looked amused if anything, but he had said, 'I sold that lease so I could devote more time to Raspberry Hill. You choose a honeymoon, then.'

She'd gazed at him with a frown. Then, 'No, thank you. I'll leave it up to you!' She'd walked away.

Consequently, she now had no idea what lay before her in more ways than one. So, despite the success of the reception, she was a little distracted and it was Justin who drew her attention to something that had escaped her.

'Way to go, Mel!' he enthused. 'I hope you'll let me drive it.'

'Drive what?'

He raised his eyes heavenwards and drew her around to the front of the car. 'Look at that.'

'What?'

'The registration, dummy!'

Mel obeyed and blinked. The registration plate said 'MEL 1'. 'What...do you mean...?' she stammered and turned to Etienne.

'All yours.' He pulled a silver, diamond-studded keyring in the shape of an M from his pocket and put it in her hand.

'I can't accept this,' she protested.

'Mel!' Justin looked horrified.

'No! It's...I mean...'

'It's your wedding present,' Etienne murmured smoothly. 'It is an accepted custom.'

'It is not! This must have cost thousands—'

'Try a hundred of them,' Justin put in airily.

'And I haven't got you anything— How many?' Mel swung towards Justin with her eyes wide.

'Sis—'

'Justin,' Etienne said firmly, 'butt out, will you?' He took the keyring still sitting in Mel's palm back. 'I'll drive until you get the hang of it,' he added to Mel and opened the nearside door. 'After you, Mrs Hurst.'

'But—'

'I don't think it's a good idea to have our first domestic here and now,' he said softly and at the same time Mrs Bedwell surged up and took Mel in her arms.

'You lucky, lucky girl,' she crooned—also tipsy, Mel decided.

Then Tosh and Ewan were on the pavement, both obviously in transports over the car.

'Will you drive us to school in it, Mel—please?' Tosh begged.

'No one, *no one*,' Ewan emphasised with awe, 'in the whole bloody district has one of these.'

'Don't swear,' Mel said automatically, 'and I think it would be a good idea if you three, all of you,' she included Mrs Bedwell in her glance around, 'sobered up!'

'Why don't you take her away, Etienne,' Justin suggested, 'before she spoils a good party?'

'I will take her away but only because I want her to myself,' Etienne replied with a grin. 'But if I were you, I'd take the last part of her advice. In you get, Mel.'

Mel hesitated but by now there were all sorts of people on the pavement enthusing over the car and what a lucky young bride she was! So she climbed in reluctantly, then she got out and kissed the boys and

Mrs Bedwell warmly, and, reluctantly, got in again. They drove away in another shower of confetti.

'I hope they'll be all right.' She looked back anxiously.

'They'll be fine.'

She turned to Etienne. 'How can you know that?'

'Mary Lees is going to see that they get home safe and sound.'

Mel subsided. 'You don't leave anything to chance, do you?'

He considered. 'Not normally.'

'I can't think of one single instance lately,' she said crossly.

'I didn't plan on you being upset about the car.'

Mel allowed a mile to elapse in silence. Etienne had changed into buff trousers and a tweed sports jacket. As the car ate up the tree-shade dappled road in the late-afternoon sunlight, he looked relaxed but very worldly.

'It didn't occur to you,' she asked cautiously, 'that I might feel—bought?'

He flicked her a glance. 'Do you?'

'I'm asking you, Etienne.'

'Mel,' he changed gear as they climbed a hill with the flick of a wrist, 'what would *you* consider suitable repayment for your delectable but reluctant body?'

Her eyes nearly fell out on stalks.

'After all,' he continued smoothly, 'you did say you realised that the time must come when we would sleep together, leaving me, apart from anything else, to gather that the prospect didn't fill you with much joy.'

She opened and closed her mouth several times but nothing came out.

'Not,' he looked at her wryly, 'that I hadn't guessed it, although you don't seem to mind me kissing you.'

'Etienne—' Speech came to her at last. 'This is still a marriage of convenience. You're not in love with me and vice versa, so somehow or other we'll have to accommodate that side of marriage but—'

'Precisely,' he broke in. 'And, as a way of making you feel better about it, I thought you might like to have a nice car to drive.'

'You freely admit you thought that?' She regarded him with astonishment.

He shrugged. 'That's what marriages of convenience are about, give and take.'

'That's what all marriages are about, I suspect,' she replied tartly, 'but you seem to be doing all the giving here.'

'At the moment.' He looked at her briefly but long enough to send a shiver down her spine because it was one of *those* looks and left her in no doubt of how he meant the balance of give and take to be set.

'But you knew what it was all about, Mel, and,' he paused and flicked her a glance with a glint of something she didn't recognise in his eyes this time, 'I do have my pride.'

She blinked. 'I don't understand.'

'I'd rather not have my wife driving around in a battered old utility about to fall apart.'

'I don't believe I'm saying this,' Mel smoothed the pale grey leather seat with a flash of humour in her eyes, 'but how far could this car be from a new ute, which, I do admit, I need?'

'So you wouldn't have any reservations about a new ute?' he came back swiftly.

'I didn't say that. But I guess your part of the bargain, as I saw it, was getting Raspberry Hill back on its feet and keeping the boys happy and on the right track, not showering me with wildly expensive presents.'

'Then you'll just have to learn to live with it.'

He slowed the car and pulled into a lay-by. 'Do you or do you not like to live a little dangerously at times?'

'I...if I have that reputation, it's a bit misleading.'

He got out and came round to her side, opening the door. She looked up at him questioningly.

'Have a drive, Mel. And to allay your fears all I expect in return at this stage is a pleasant companion.'

Mel looked at the walnut dash, the silver spokes of the steering wheel and she breathed in the new leather. And discovered that her fingers were itching, her feet could feel the pedals beneath them. She'd been driving since she was twelve, only on the property until she got her licence, but she was experienced, good at it and knew enough about cars to appreciate the mechanical marvels of this one, not to mention its style and elegance.

'Oh, OK.' She got out and walked round to the driver's side.

Etienne got in and leaned forward to adjust the driver's seat. 'Try that.'

She fitted herself into the seat and marvelled at the comfort of it compared to her ute—she'd had to import a cushion to the ute to protect her bottom from springs sticking up. And she put her hands on the steering wheel but had to sit forward a bit, so he told her how to move the back of the seat forward.

'That feels fine, thanks. Well, here goes!' She switched the motor on and drove out of the lay-by, then looked at him comically. 'Where are we going?'

He named a luxury resort south of Yeppoon, adding, 'For two nights, then we're off to Great Keppel Island—I hope you approve?'

This time she read the glint in his eyes accurately—sheer wicked amusement.

'How nice,' she said. 'I love Keppel! Why blue?'

He raised an eyebrow.

Mel took a hand off the steering wheel and gestured towards the bonnet beyond the windscreen. 'I was wondering why you chose blue.'

'To match your eyes.'

Mel's fingers tightened on the wheel. 'Oh. Thanks.'

'My pleasure.'

She made a frustrated little sound as the power of the car flowed through her fingertips. 'Thank you very much. I'll take great care of it. I'm sorry I haven't got anything for you.' She gestured. 'I mean, cufflinks or—whatever brides give their bridegrooms.'

His lips twisted. 'Never mind. You can always rectify that on our first wedding anniversary. Incidentally, just so that we don't go through this all over again, I—bought you some clothes.'

Mel took both hands off the steering wheel to throw them in the air. 'I give up!' She grabbed the wheel again. 'Do I dress badly enough to affect your pride in your wife?'

'It's not that. I have no problem with your taste.

But,' he paused, 'you might need some more clothes, that's all.'

'All,' she muttered darkly.

'You can take them back and change them if you want to.'

'On a Saturday afternoon?'

He grinned. 'Well, maybe not.'

'Have you any more confessions to make, Etienne?'

'No.'

'Just as well—oh, is that the turn-off?'

'Yep, we're almost there.'

'Good, because, and believe me, it's the first time I've ever said this, but I need a drink.'

'I'll join you in that. It's the first time I've ever got married too.'

She regarded him gravely then a reluctant smile curved her lips. 'Join the club.'

They had a bure overlooking the beach and the waters of Keppel Bay. The roof was steep and thatched with no ceiling, the walls dark wood and the whole ambiance was exotic.

'Like being nestled in a Javanese jungle hideaway,' Mel commented. 'Oh, wow! Look at this!'

'This' was an indoor pool and spa, set amongst pebbles, lush plants and some exquisite statues.

Further inspection revealed a bedroom with a four-poster bed draped with turquoise and silver hangings.

And Mel discovered that not only did she have new clothes but also new luggage, in the form of a blue-to-match-the-car roller suitcase. Next to it, her suit-case from her boarding-school days looked shabby.

She grimaced and wished devoutly that she hadn't decided to be quite so unconventional a bride and splurged a bit, thereby saving herself this embarrassment.

Not that there was much to splurge, she reminded herself. But before she opened the new case, in fact she was looking around a bit dazedly, Etienne put a glass of champagne in her hand and drew her out onto the veranda.

'More of this and who knows?' She attempted to look whimsical.

'You were the only member of the family who didn't tuck into the champers at the reception,' he remarked. 'It's nice here, isn't it?'

She sank down into a chair. The sun was setting, and even in an area renowned for fabulous sunsets, it was a beauty. All the colours of the rainbow were layered across the sky and reflected in the waters. Great Keppel and North Keppel Islands were a deep, misty blue and as she watched the sea turned to violet as the colours slowly faded from the sky.

She thought suddenly of Raspberry Hill, not that far away as the crow flew, and how she had a favourite spot on the headland where she often watched the sun set. And it came to her that Raspberry Hill was safe but above all the boys were *safe*, so whatever price she had to pay was worth it.

She took a sip of champagne, then another and looked across at Etienne. 'Cheers.' She raised her glass. 'To us!'

He raised his glass in reply. 'To us, Mel. Feeling better?'

She nodded and drained her glass. 'I might even

get ready for dinner. Or,' she paused, 'are honey-mooners expected to dine in on their wedding night?'

'Honeymooners can do what they like. I don't know about you but I'm starving and I know they serve a wonderful flambéd grill here, so let's try the restaurant.'

'You know, I hardly ate a thing at the reception! Yes, let's.'

'Off you go, then.'

Her new clothes were beautiful.

Obviously expensive, lovely fabrics and colours, and if he'd chosen them himself, she paused to think, he'd had some experience at this. She dug down into the bag and there was underwear as well; gossamer silks, satins and lace, bras, bikini briefs, nightgowns, the lot. Even four pairs of the finest pantihose, black, pale grey and two beige, still in their packets. There was also a set of luxury cosmetics.

She stared down at it all, at the exquisite colours, coffee and cream, lemon and white, French navy, peach, ivory, and pulled her hand away suddenly. She closed the suitcase, stood it against the wall and went to sit in an armchair.

This was too much, she decided. Raspberry Hill and the boys might be safe but accepting and wearing his choice of clothes, and particularly underwear, would be the equivalent of turning herself into a mail-order bride. Into the kind of woman *he* wanted, not the kind of woman she was.

And she knew herself well enough to know that, however she finally went to Etienne's bed, it could only be as herself, not some sexy creature dolled up in his choice of silks and satins.

So, once more tense and unsure of how to go on, she didn't change. She washed her hands, touched up her minimal make-up and presented herself in the lounge, still wearing her lime trouser suit—which was perfectly suitable anyway. Etienne was watching the news on television.

He looked up almost absently then stood up with a question in his eyes.

'Uh—' Mel hesitated '—I decided to draw the line at the clothes. There's nothing wrong with this outfit, is there?'

'Not at all, but what's wrong with the clothes?'

Mel fiddled with her wedding ring then looked down at it, to find another cause for dissatisfaction that had been simmering away at the back of her mind since he'd slid it onto her finger.

She'd declined an engagement ring and expected a plain gold band for the wedding ring. In fact, that was what she'd been fitted for. What had eventuated was quite different. A broad gold band with beautifully chased edges and a stunning diamond set into it. If any ring could be called an engagement and wedding ring combined, this one could—yet another example of Etienne getting his own way.

'There's nothing wrong with the clothes. I just wouldn't feel comfortable wearing them. This may be hard for you to understand,' she continued, 'but wearing things chosen for you by a man you barely know is, well, it makes you feel like a mail-order bride.' She tilted her chin at him.

'I didn't choose them.'

Her eyes widened. 'Who, then?'

'Mary Lees and Mrs Bedwell.'

Mel opened her mouth to express herself colourfully then closed it. 'I should have known!' she said instead.

'Yes. Well. Does it make you feel any better to know I have no idea what's in that suitcase?'

Mel considered. 'It was still your idea.'

'It wasn't. Mrs Bedwell came to me and told me you were being difficult on the subject of a trousseau.'

This time Mel did express herself colourfully. 'All the same, you *paid* for them,' she added.

He shrugged.

Mel heaved a frustrated sigh. 'They're so…they're like nothing I've worn in my life!'

He raised his eyebrows. 'I would have thought Mary had good taste.'

'I don't mean the clothes, they're lovely. It's the underwear. And I don't mean they're not lovely but when you usually buy your underwear at the supermarket and prefer cotton anyway—do you see what I mean?'

'You would hate it if I told you what I do see, Mel,' he drawled, 'so before this conversation becomes too much of a trial, you wear whatever you like and perhaps we should go to dinner?'

'Oh.' She looked downwards unwittingly and colour mounted in her cheeks at the thought of him seeing beneath her clothes to her underwear. 'I…' She looked up to encounter a particularly wicked look in his eyes. 'I agree,' she said with hauteur.

CHAPTER SEVEN

THEY walked down to the restaurant, which opened, through tall diamond-paned doors, onto a garden then the beach. A burgundy and deep blue colour scheme complemented the sheen of crystal and silver, and candles lit the tables. The *maître d'* hurried forward and welcomed them by name.

'Mr and Mrs Hurst,' he said delightedly, turning to Mel and bowing. 'Ma'am, this is a great pleasure. May I pass on my, and all the staff's, felicitations? We're really honoured to have you here on your wedding night.'

'Thank you,' Mel said, somewhat taken aback. 'How did you know?'

'Word spreads fast!' He winked conspiratorially. 'Please come this way; I've prepared our best table for you.'

The restaurant's best table was a banquette in a secluded corner with a lovely view through the doors to the beach and the now silvery waters beyond as a moon rose.

They sat opposite each other, cocooned in the plush candlelit burgundy banquette, and the starched pink damask tablecloth was strewn with little silver horseshoes and wedding bells.

'I detect more than news travelling fast here,' she said humorously. 'Mary Lees again?'

'She did make all the bookings. So, what will it be?'

Mel consulted the menu, changed her mind a couple of times then settled for what he ordered. And she chattered inconsequently while they waited. Etienne seemed happy enough to allow her to direct the flow of conversation along harmless lines.

He'd changed into a black shirt and trousers with his sports jacket and he looked powerful but laid-back. As if this wedding night was not at all momentous for him, she reflected, and she stopped making conversation rather suddenly.

Fortunately, all the accoutrements for their meal arrived at about the same time. A trolley, under the command of the *maître d'*, drew up beside the table, laden with copper-lined chafing dishes piled with glistening green olives, grilled bacon and kidneys, onions and parsley and two fillets of steak.

And, with ceremony, the contents of each chafing dish were added to the flambé dish to bubble gently before the brandy was poured on and set alight. The blue-gold flame hovered briefly and the most delicious aroma arose.

It was the best grill Mel had ever eaten and definitely an experience that didn't need to be talked through.

She put her knife and fork together at last and patted her stomach. 'Mmm…mmm!'

'You were hungry,' he teased.

'I haven't really eaten well for a week.' She paused and looked embarrassed.

The teasing light died out of his eyes. 'That worried about marrying me, Mel?'

She hesitated and chose her words with care. 'Most brides probably have some nerves, although,' she tipped a hand, 'maybe not these days.'

'Maybe not,' he agreed. 'Most, even traditional brides, are a little more used to their husbands than you are, however.'

'I know what you mean,' she said slowly. 'As a matter of fact I rather regretted imposing those restrictions on us before the wedding. Not, well, I guess, not morally is a good way of putting it, but because it made things harder. It's certainly made this night harder, anyway— Oh, thank you!' She took the dessert menu being offered to her.

He waited until the waiter had left. 'That's an interesting way of putting it—we are very properly and morally married, Mel.'

'We may be but not really for the right reasons. Mind you,' she looked rueful, 'I didn't mean to bring that up. One thing I can honestly tell you about being married to you, Etienne, is that I don't seem to know if I'm on my head or my heels. Actually,' she confided, 'and I don't know if this is champagne and a good meal talking, but today has been—I feel as if I've been on a roller coaster all day.'

'So there have been "ups"?' he queried.

She ran her finger down the menu and it hovered over the pavlova but moved on.

'There have,' she said thoughtfully. 'I can't make up my mind between the pavlova or the lemon tart.'

'Have them both since you haven't eaten for a

week, just don't keep me in suspense, Mel,' he drawled and added specifically, 'about the "ups".'

'Oh. Well, I walked down the aisle feeling quite pleased with myself whereas I walked up it wondering what on earth I was getting myself into. Then I found myself enjoying the reception although I have no idea why. *Then*—I was really upset about being given a luxury car but thoroughly enjoyed driving it, and I watched the sun set thinking that the boys were safe and so was Raspberry Hill so it all had to be worth it, only to get upset again over some clothes. Strange, isn't it?'

But her blue eyes were alight with humour and shining in a way they hadn't all day, and certainly not over the gift of a luxury car, Etienne found himself thinking. And he went on to reflect on the irony of having married the one girl his fortune meant nothing to.

'How was your day?' she asked, breaking into his thoughts.

'It too had its ups and downs. You were ten minutes late and I was quite sure you'd got cold feet. Then you accused me of making you feel "bought" and like a mail-order bride, and for a horrible moment I thought you were going to invite the whole family on this honeymoon.'

She laughed. 'I doubt if I'd have been able to tear them away! But—were there any "ups"?'

His lips twisted. 'Two. Watching you walk down the aisle looking so beautiful and so Mel Ethridge at the same time, and kissing you.'

Mel sat back. 'I'll have the pavlova, thank you, although I shouldn't.'

'Then I have a better idea: let's go for a walk.'

She took a little breath as his eyes lingered on her mouth. 'So—you could kiss me?' she hazarded.

'Well,' his eyes glinted, 'I don't think it would be a good idea for me to get rusty and too out of practice.'

She hesitated with a half-smile on her lips.

'Besides which,' he continued, 'one of the reasons for one of your ''ups''—walking down the aisle feeling pleased with yourself—may, just *may*, I say,' he warned, 'have had something to do with what happened in the moments before you waltzed down the aisle.'

'I...I'm a fast walker,' she warned in turn.

'Then I'll just have to prove that I'm a fast worker, won't I?' He stood up.

Mel stared into his eyes then put her napkin on the table and followed suit.

But once outside, they discovered that the weather had changed. The moon was obscured by clouds and there was lightning in the air. So it was not only dark but also deserted and the sea was also dark as it broke against the shore, not a fierce surf but enough to add the tang of salt to the air.

Etienne hesitated and looked at the sky. 'This may not be such a good idea; I think it's going to rain.'

Right on cue thunder grumbled, although not that close.

'I don't mind a bit of rain,' she said and stopped to listen. 'What was that?'

'I don't know.' He stood with his head back and listened himself.

The thread of sound came again.

'It's an animal,' she said, 'in distress. We'd better have a look; I think it's coming from over there.' She pointed towards a thick patch of bushland beside the beach.

'Mel,' he said but she ignored him and started to run towards the sound. He swore, and followed her.

What they found was a stray calf caught up in a barbed-wire fence, exhausted by its struggles, but only after they'd ploughed through almost impenetrable bush and been soaked by the first shower of the evening.

'We may need help,' he said.

'We may not have time,' she answered with rain streaming off her face and flattening her hair. 'He could die!'

'I doubt it but—all right.' He pulled off his jacket and put it over her shoulders. Half an hour later, with a herculean effort and her help, he managed to release the calf, and with surprising energy it bounded off into the bush.

'Oh, well done,' Mel breathed. 'But now it'll be lost! Should we—?'

'No, Mel, we should not. Listen!'

Above the rain, they heard a full-blooded moo answered by a miniature moo some distance apart but getting closer to each other. 'I would say a family reunion is about to take place.'

'Thank heavens!'

'I do agree and let's get out of this bloody rain.' He looked down at himself rather comically.

Mel did the same. 'We're ruined—oh, my poor shoes!—but you were wonderful, Etienne.'

They started to laugh together.

When they were back in the comfort of their bure he told her to take a shower before they had a spa but reaction had set in and Mel was shivering uncontrollably. So he picked her up and carried her into the bedroom.

'I—I—I'm sorry,' she said through chattering teeth. 'I expect I've well and truly ruined our wedding night.'

He set her on her feet and looked down at her wryly. 'I think we might give up on this one.' He picked her up again and sat her down on the end of the bed. 'But listen, Mel,' he said softly and took her chin in his fingers so she had to look up at him, 'on the subject of our wedding night, the last thing I want to feel is that I'm taking you against your will. The last thing I want *you* to feel is that it's something you have to get over and done with.'

She sniffed and licked her lips.

'And,' he went on, 'I'd just like to point out a couple of things; while I'm not going to force you into anything, we have to start somewhere but it so happens—that "somewhere" is already established. I've told you how I feel and I know you're not unmoved either.'

He dropped his hand but his eyes searched hers.

She nodded slowly.

'Then,' he touched her face again lightly, 'we have that in common plus a whole lot more. Believe me, we can build well.'

He trailed his fingers down her cheek in a way that was mesmerising to Mel. They made her skin feel like silk and she broke out in goose-pimples that spread down towards her breasts and caused her nipples to tingle. *He* made her tremble inwardly, the whole tall, damp, strong, dark length of him.

It crossed Mel's overwrought mind to tell him how much she'd liked the feel of his arms around her, and the easy strength that allowed him to pick her up and put her down at whim. It crossed her mind to say that the one way she could visualise falling asleep tonight would be in the sanctuary of his arms and that one part of her longed to leave all the decision-making up to him.

But the words wouldn't be said. He waited for a moment then he broke the contact and turned away. 'See you in the pool.'

He'd activated the spa by the time she came out of the bedroom in her one-piece blue swimsuit, and there was a silver tray with two cream-topped dark drinks in long glasses beside it. Flickering, very soft, concealed lighting added to the exotic, jungle feel.

'Join me,' he invited from amidst the steam and bubbles. 'I have to tell you, this is exactly what you need after battling the elements, barbed wire and strayed calves.'

Mel grimaced and slid into the water. 'What's this?' She indicated the glasses.

'Irish coffee. Renowned for its sleep-giving properties but also delicious.'

'Mmm.' She picked up her glass and sipped. 'Yum!' She closed her eyes and allowed her body to relax under the heated jets of bubbles.

'By the way, I rang home,' he said. 'They're all fine, quite sober now, although Justin is nursing a sore behind.'

Mel blinked. 'Why?'

'Your beloved Rimfire took exception to your absence and got a sly bite in while he was being fed. Justin has therefore relinquished the chore to Mrs Bedwell and he asked me to pass on the message that the next time you rescue any damn horses, please make sure they're not man eaters.'

Mel broke out into spontaneous laughter. 'I was afraid of that!' she gurgled. 'I warned Rimfire not to bite the hand that fed him. He obviously didn't listen to me.'

'Why does he hate men?'

'Some man was terribly cruel to him, I guess. Do you ride, Etienne?'

'I used to as a kid but I haven't for years. Why?'

'I wondered if you'd enjoy riding around Raspberry Hill, that's all.'

'I would,' he said slowly. 'Do you have a horse for me?'

'No. Justin is only into mechanical forms of transport at the moment, Ewan was never into horses and

Tosh has a pony, that's all.' She sat up, obviously struck by a thought. 'I could get you one.'

'I could get my own.'

'No, no,' she waved a hand, 'I'm sure I could find one that—'

'Not one that you'll feel obligated to ride into the council chambers, or one that's liable to bite and kick me, please,' he broke in with mock-alarm.

She grinned at him. 'Not at all. But there are always people with horses to give away because they can't afford to feed them or whatever. And I thought,' she drew an excited breath, 'if I brought it up to scratch, made sure it was well-trained et cetera, et cetera—I could give it to you as a wedding present.'

He was leaning back with his arms spread out along the edge of the pool and his dark eyes softened at her eager expression, the way her hair was curling riotously so that she looked about twelve. 'Thank you. I look forward to it.'

Mel finished her Irish coffee, and hiccuped.

'I would say all this alcohol is finally getting to me!'

'OK. Next part of the cure.' He got up and left the pool. In a pair of charcoal board shorts there was little left to Mel's imagination and it was hard not to look awestruck. He was tanned and well-proportioned and you could see where that excellent co-ordination came from, finely tuned muscles, long legs and wide, powerful shoulders.

There was a pile of thirsty turquoise towels on a stool and he dried himself off briefly then reached down a hand to her. 'Out you get.'

She came out with his help and was wrapped in a towel.

'Get dry, get into your supermarket pyjamas or whatever you normally wear, get into bed and listen to the rain. I'll sleep out here.' He dropped a light kiss on her curls and put her away from him.

'Will you be comfortable?'

He pointed to a divan in the main section of the lounge. 'That's also a bed; I'll be fine. And so will you, Mel,' he said firmly. But a sudden smile twisted his lips. 'Tomorrow is another day, OK?'

'OK,' she echoed and hesitated. 'Thanks. For everything.'

'My pleasure.'

She thought he said it with an undertone of dryness and flinched inwardly but out of nowhere an uncontrollable yawn overtook her.

He laughed softly, patted her on the bottom and turned away.

Feeling rather foolish but definitely exhausted, Mel was more than happy to seek the solace of the bedroom. She changed into her pyjamas and climbed into the huge bed almost too tired to switch off the bedside lamp. Then she paused with her hand on the switch, and her last thought of the day, as rain hammered on the windows, was that whatever happened from now on, somehow she would make him understand that her reservations were neither childish nor foolish...

She didn't wake up until about eight-thirty—most unusual for her. At first she had no idea where she was, even thought she might be dreaming. Maybe a…concubine, she mused, and stretched luxuriously, in some sultan's palace, awaiting her lord who was tall and dark with curly hair and the absolute master of her body…

She sat up abruptly as the thatched roof and four-poster bed with its turquoise and silver hangings fell into place. So did her cotton nightshirt with a zebra on the front—some concubine, she thought drily.

She lay back and hugged her pillow while she experienced a little pang at the memory of her wedding day, a day she may not have handled that well.

All she could hear was the wind and the surf as her thoughts drifted on and it came to her that she was in deep trouble.

Something was holding her back from surrendering to Etienne. Something ridiculous? she pondered. Since he'd taken to invading her daydreams in the most embarrassing way, many might agree, she conceded. However, the fact remained that, while he might want her, he didn't love her and she just didn't seem able to get over that hurdle.

Then she tossed away the bedclothes and went to take a shower.

When she came back into the bedroom, the blue roller suitcase seemed to leap up and shout at her but she gave it a long, thoughtful look and turned away to get her newest jeans and a favourite blouse out of her old case.

'Is this continuing as you mean to go on?'

She asked the question of herself as she sat down in front of the mirror to rub some moisturiser into her face and brush her hair.

'I have no idea,' she replied to her image. 'Something—*something* keeps holding me back from those clothes as well as the rest of it and perhaps all I can do is try to explain it to him?'

She put her brush down and regarded herself more thoroughly than she was accustomed to. No problem with her hair, it did its own thing, which seemed to be quite acceptable. So were her blouse and jeans. She got up then paused to contemplate her figure. But that brought back memories of Etienne in his board shorts for some reason, so she tossed her head, bit one of her nails briefly and ventured beyond the bedroom.

To find that breakfast was waiting for her.

'Not a good day,' Etienne said after greeting her casually.

'No,' she agreed, unfurling her napkin. 'Not that I heard it but it looks as if a solid storm came this way last night.'

She glanced outside to see that the palm trees in the garden were still bending and waving their fronds around beneath a grey sky, although it wasn't raining.

'Several storms.' Etienne served himself up bacon and eggs while she selected fresh fruit and yoghurt to start. 'Let's hope it clears up. I gather you slept well?'

She received his probing glance with all the serenity she could muster. 'Like a log. How about you?'

'I woke up a couple of times.' He poured some coffee.

Mel closed her eyes and breathed in. 'That smells divine!'

He poured her a cup and pushed it over to her. 'What would you like to do today?'

Mel glanced across at him. In jeans and a grey T-shirt he looked big, vital and somewhat impatient, as if he couldn't wait to get out and about and doing things.

'I have no idea what we can do in this weather,' she said slowly, 'unless they have a gym here?'

For a moment, he went quite still with a piece of toast poised halfway to his mouth. Then he started to laugh.

'Have I said something funny?' But threaded through her puzzlement was a trace of alarm.

'Yes and no,' he responded, still grinning.

'Well, tell me!' A spark of indignation lit her eyes.

'You won't like it,' he warned.

'How can you know?'

He shrugged. 'The thing is, I never suspected that I would have to spend the first day of my married life—letting off steam in a gym, Mel.'

She blushed scarlet. 'I…just…that just came out,' she tried to explain.

'Things that "just come out",' he drawled, 'are often indicative of a state of mind.'

She took a sip of her coffee and tried to regroup as he finished his bacon and eggs.

'I guess I haven't thought much about your side of things, I'm sorry. Other,' she confessed with honesty as well as seeing an opening to explain her feelings to him, 'than to wonder what you see in me as opposed to all the women who have been gossiped about in connection with you.'

'Ah, gossip.' He sat back and pushed away his plate. 'I would have thought you of all people would understand the pitfalls of gossip.'

'Why?'

He got up and roamed about a bit then propped himself against the door frame and folded his arms. 'Take this scenario. According to gossip, you, Mel Ethridge, are a loose cannon at times. You go about creating all sorts of drama, some people see you as seriously nutty, others see you as even lacking a gene.'

Mel slammed her napkin down on the table then forced herself to take a steadying breath and achieve calm reasonableness at the same time.

He raised an eyebrow. 'I seem to have made my point.'

'No, you have not!' Calm reasonableness flew out of the window. 'I don't know where you got them from but its common *knowledge* you've had any number of elegant, sophisticated, gorgeous lovers, none of whom were impoverished, *nutty*, nineteen-year-olds!'

'Then I'm obviously due for a change,' he drawled and shot out a hand to field the, fortunately closed, little bottle of marmalade she flung at him. 'Now, now, Mel,' he warned softly but dangerously. 'What do you want me to believe, that the gossip about you is wrong or all too accurate?'

'I don't care what you believe.' She squared her shoulders and tilted her chin at him.

'I wish you wouldn't do that,' he murmured with what appeared to be a lightning change of mood.

She blinked at him.

Play the **Lucky Hearts** *Game*

and get...

2 FREE BOOKS
and a **FREE MYSTERY GIFT...**

Yes! **YOURS to KEEP!**

I have scratched off the silver card. Please send me my *2 FREE BOOKS* and *FREE mystery GIFT*. I understand that I am under no obligation to purchase any books as explained on the back of this card.

Scratch Here!

then look below to see what your cards get you... 2 Free Books & a Free Mystery Gift!

306 HDL DU6W

106 HDL DU7E

FIRST NAME

LAST NAME

ADDRESS

APT.#

CITY

STATE/PROV.

ZIP/POSTAL CODE

(H-P-08/03)

Twenty-one gets you
2 FREE BOOKS
and a *FREE MYSTERY GIFT!*

Twenty gets you
2 FREE BOOKS!

Nineteen gets you
1 FREE BOOK!

TRY AGAIN!

'It doesn't matter.' He shrugged. 'Do you play golf?'

'I... What's that got to do with it?'

'As a way of defusing this situation, I thought we might have a game of golf. They have a nine-hole course here. I brought my clubs; we could hire some for you so long as you don't mind a bit of wind.'

'I was only trying to explain...' She hesitated.

'Your reservations about me?' He raised an eyebrow. 'Maybe you should have done that before we got married.'

'Maybe I should,' she retorted then bit her lip. 'Yes, I used to play golf with my father, as a matter of fact.'

'Then let's get to it.'

She stood up and eyed him, sincerely regretting this impasse and her part in it, but really, she thought, he had offered the first insult.

'I'll get a jacket.'

CHAPTER EIGHT

IN THE event, they were able to make up a four-ball game with another couple staying at the resort.

At first, Mel thought this would be a good idea in light of the less than amiable vibes between her and Etienne but she was soon to change her mind.

'Ah, the honeymooners!' Brad Littleby greeted them on being introduced. 'This is my wife, Paula.'

'How do you do?' Mel murmured.

Paula, in her middle twenties, was a ravishing redhead, expensively kitted out in all the right attire down to her tan and white golf shoes and matching glove. Paula, as it turned out, was also a person who spoke her mind.

'Thought you might be taking it easy this morning,' she said to Mel with a knowing little look that grated on her. 'Wedding night and all that!'

'Mel has a lot of energy,' Etienne murmured. 'Don't you, sweetheart?'

Mel debated briefly on how to respond and found herself still feeling that she'd been misunderstood over breakfast and not only that but also on edge, so she settled for 'in kind'.

'It would take a lot more than getting married to sink me,' she said coolly, and walked towards the first tee swinging her driver.

* * *

The course ran alongside the beach in places, fringed with casuarina trees that sighed in the breeze. As it was, not too arduous and well-kept, the worst that could happen to a ball was to bury itself in a sand dune if it was hooked or sliced. This happened to Paula, who was swooped upon by a pair of anxious plovers guarding a nest.

Etienne happened to be closest to her at the time and got called in to defend her from the birds.

Mel watched this little bit of byplay and decided that if she was any judge, Paula Littleby was the kind of woman who would respond to any attractive man despite the presence of her husband and his wife. She guessed that Brad Littleby, who was short and portly but rather nice, would be close to forty and she gained the impression that he and Paula hadn't been married that long themselves.

Whatever else she might find difficult to cope with—such as a so-far fake marriage in front of strangers and a woman on the prowl, she thought drily—her game of golf hadn't deserted her, she was happy to discover, however.

'You're pretty good,' Etienne said at one stage when she'd sunk a three-metre putt. He himself played off a four handicap.

'Thank you!' Her cheeks were glowing despite her mental turmoil. 'Mind you,' she confided, 'I'm seriously on my mettle.' She looked across at Paula.

Etienne followed her gaze. 'Surely—you wouldn't be jealous, Mel?'

'Not at all!' Mel denied but kicking herself at the same time for falling into such an obvious trap. 'I...I—' she shrugged and plucked a reason for what she'd said out of thin air '—I just don't appreciate wedding-night cracks.'

He grinned. 'You might—one day.'

'When I do, if I do, I'll let you know, Etienne,' she responded, now thoroughly annoyed with him as well as disliking Paula Littleby.

'So you're prim and proper as well as being a right little "do-gooder",' he drawled.

If only you knew about the concubine, the wood nymph and the strange girl with the cheetah cub, she thought, but said instead, 'Possibly.' She shrugged. 'They're waiting for you,' she pointed out.

For some reason Etienne, who had been brilliant on the greens until then, three-putted the hole.

If Paula detected her disapproval she gave no sign of it, and Mel had no choice but to fall in with the suggestion, made after the game, that they have dinner together that night.

'And what would you like to do now?' Etienne asked her courteously, after they'd had lunch.

'Be a million miles away from here,' Mel muttered not quite beneath her breath, as she thought of the disaster of the morning and the evening ahead.

He stared at her then simply got up and walked away.

Nor did he return to their bure until half-past five in the afternoon, by which time, if it hadn't been for the fact that he had the keys to her new car on him, she was in such a state of tension she would have driven herself home.

She stood up apprehensively as he let himself in. Despite her going for a long walk then having a swim from the beach—the weather had cleared—the afternoon had been interminable for her.

'So.' He put the diamond-studded keyring on the table. 'Still caught up with all the evils of your situation, not to mention being a right little prig, Mel?'

She was immediately tempted to explain that she was no such thing, that things simply had got out of hand, but she cleared her throat instead. 'I didn't mean to be but perhaps,' she conceded, 'having to act out a part in front of strangers was...a bit much.'

'We have a week to get through in front of strangers,' he pointed out.

'It mightn't be so bad,' she said cautiously, 'if everyone didn't know we were on our honeymoon.'

'On the contrary, we could solve the whole problem if we cancelled this honeymoon and went home,' he said harshly.

Mel swallowed painfully. 'But that would...I mean, the boys and everyone at home would...' She broke off and flinched as he softly but fluently consigned the whole population of Raspberry Hill to hell.

She began to shake inwardly because it was all so difficult—more than she'd dreamt possible. Well, she amended the thought, she'd been unable to dwell on the problems of her honeymoon; there'd been a wall in her thoughts, hadn't there? All the same, it *had* come as a shock to discover there was also a wall in her heart that refused to allow her to take the final step towards becoming Etienne's wife...

'Look,' he picked up the keyring and threw it up in the air a couple of times, 'can we just establish one thing, Mel? Do you ever intend to go to bed with me—or not?'

Her throat worked.

'Because there's no point in going on otherwise. There's no point in wading our way through a sham honeymoon then still having the difficulty of going back to Raspberry Hill. Where you're obviously worried about what the boys are going to think.'

'What are you suggesting?' she asked hoarsely.

'An annulment,' he said flatly. 'Then you could go your own way, Mel.'

From somewhere she dragged up the composure to deal with this.

'You have all the cards in your hands, Etienne. I don't have any. For what it's worth, I assumed I would be able to do this but I just can't seem to—' she rubbed her face wearily '—at the moment I just can't seem to square it with...I don't know...maybe just the person I *am*. I'm sorry. But if you could give me a little leeway, I'd like to keep trying.'

He didn't respond, at least not verbally. Instead, he looked her up and down with so much cynicism she felt herself shrivel beneath it.

Then he spoke at last. 'How about tonight? Shall I cancel dinner with Brad and Paula?'

'No. I mean—no. I'll—be fine.'

He looked at his watch. 'Then you have an hour to get ready. I'm going for a swim.'

'Where...where have you been?' she asked.

'To see a man about a dog,' he replied briefly and stripped off his shirt. Then he gathered a towel and his board shorts, and walked out.

Once again, as she walked into the bedroom, the blue roller suitcase seemed to jump up and shout at her.

She walked over to it and gave it serious consideration. Then she sat down on the bed with her hands in her lap and gave the whole situation serious consideration.

Had she awakened a sleeping tiger in Etienne Hurst?

Certainly a formidable opponent, she thought with a tremor of nerves. On the other hand, he was the one who'd given her no option but to marry him.

Her shoulders sagged because, of course, that wasn't quite true. In essence, she'd made a bargain and was not holding up her side of it. Then, out of nowhere, it occurred to her that part of her problem today had been the proximity of just the kind of glamorous, sophisticated woman she imagined Etienne should have married.

And she came to a sudden decision.

She was ready when Etienne came back from his swim, sitting, seemingly peacefully, on the veranda watching the sun set.

But she took an unexpected breath as he loomed up on the other side of the railing, almost terrifyingly attractive as well as looking damp and brisk and not to be trifled with.

She stood up.

He paused on the step. He was rubbing his hair with the towel then he slung it over his shoulder. 'Your clothes? Or mine?' he queried.

Mel looked down. She wore a shimmering pale aqua top with a smoky-grey silk skirt that billowed to mid-calf and a pair of high, barely there silver sandals. Her heavy hair was drawn back into a loose knot, with long tendrils framing her face. She'd also experimented with the cosmetics Mary Lees had provided.

'Yours,' she said.

'What brought about this change of heart?'

'I told you I'd like to keep trying.' She moved her slim shoulders and examined her wedding ring. Then her eyes met his again. 'It seemed a good way to start.'

'Well, between them, Mary Lees and Mrs Bedwell, they seem to have got the fit right.'

His dark gaze ran down her figure and Mel felt all the fine hairs on her arms stand up at the same time as she hid a spark of disappointment in her eyes by lowering her lashes. How really…wet, she marvelled, to be set on fire by a man who made that kind of mundane comment on her appearance. Come to that, how…insane to be bothered by the thought of going to bed with this man when he could set her alight just by looking her up and down. All the same, she *was*, she reminded herself.

'That would be Mrs Bedwell's part in the operation, I imagine,' she said drily. 'I now remember that certain items of my clothing—and a pair of shoes— seemed to disappear for a while then they mysteriously reappeared.'

'With no explanation?' He raised an eyebrow.

'Now I come to think of it, Batman got the blame. She told me he'd acquired the habit of squirrelling away clothes. I can't think why I didn't query the fact that he hadn't chewed any of them.'

'You had a bit on your mind.'

'Yes,' she agreed. 'I suppose I did.' She moved and

the skirt twirled. 'Would you rather I changed into something of mine?'

'Not at all—did I say that?' Some wicked amusement gleamed in his eyes.

'No. You don't seem to be visibly impressed one way or the other, though,' she said tartly.

'Oh, I am,' he replied softly. 'Not only do you look simply gorgeous, Mel, but the thought of the fight you must have had with yourself over what clothes to wear—fills me with awe too.'

By now he'd stepped onto the veranda and they were only separated by a few inches.

Mel breathed again rather unexpectedly instead of telling him to go to hell, which had been on the tip of her tongue.

'Would it be too much to ask if you were able to persuade yourself away from cotton, supermarket underwear as well?' he drawled.

To her horror, her breathing became more ragged and a dew of sweat beaded her forehead because he was so close and, despite her hurt and anger, it was impossible not to be affected. To even visualise herself in his arms in no underwear at all. Why is *that* always there, she asked herself in despair, when I'm making such a fuss about sleeping with him?

But the answer came with the man. Etienne Hurst was supremely desirable. The planes and angles of his body were so strong yet clean and fine-tuned, his shoulders so broad, but not only that, he had all the confidence of a superbly fit athlete and a man who knew women all too well, she didn't doubt.

Do I want to be just any woman to him, though? It flashed through her mind.

'Mel?'

She blushed and took a step backwards. 'Uh—you were saying?' she asked disjointedly.

'I was contemplating your underwear.'

He lifted his hand and touched her hot cheek and ripples of extreme sensuality flowed down her body, not only at the feel of his fingers on her cheek but also at the way he was looking at her. A heavy-lidded dark gaze that told her all the curves of her body, the sheen of her skin in her most private places might just as well be on parade for him.

'It's…my own,' she said with an effort.

'Good.' He took his fingers away. 'For some reason I like the thought of you preferring cotton and no frills, don't ask me why.'

She did anyway. 'Why?'

His brow creased briefly. 'Maybe there's a nun-like quality to you, Mel Ethridge.'

'I can assure you there isn't.'

'What would you know about it?' he asked with his lips twisting.

She bit her lip in confusion.

'OK!' He moved away. 'I applaud the battle you've done with yourself, Mel. Give me ten minutes and we'll go to dinner.'

As soon as Mel laid eyes on Paula Littleby she knew that, at least on one front, she'd made the right decision regarding clothes.

The redhead was looking superb in a tight black dress that showed off her cleavage and a stunning diamond necklace to full advantage and shouted couturier. Nor did Paula bother to hide the spark of surprise in her eyes as she studied Mel's outfit, although she said nothing initially.

Brad Littleby was full of compliments, however. 'Wow! The bride looks stunning! You're a lucky guy, Etienne!'

'Thank you, I know it,' Etienne murmured, whereas Mel smiled nervously then took herself to task—don't be a wimp or a prig, you can do this!

'I take it you shop in Brisbane, darling,' Paula remarked.

'As a matter of fact I have someone who does it for me,' Mel replied. 'Saves a lot of time.'

Etienne shot her an amused little glance but sobered immediately. 'Shall we go in?'

'But I adore shopping,' Paula objected, rising to her feet.

'Don't I know it?' Brad contributed ruefully.

'Most women do,' Paula said with a tinge of venom.

'Mel leads a very busy life,' Etienne contributed.

'Then I'd better take some tips from her!' Paula put her arm through Mel's. 'Because I am bored stiff with my life!'

Uh-oh, are we in the middle of a domestic here? Mel wondered.

'So, tell me what you're so busy doing you don't have time to shop?' Paula asked, once they'd been seated at the same table Mel and Etienne had shared the night before, although tonight there were no wedding bells and horseshoes.

Mel fingered her napkin and explained about Raspberry Hill and her three brothers.

'And you never wanted to do anything else?' Paula looked amazed.

'Not really.' Mel smiled. 'I guess I was born and bred a country girl.'

'Then how did you meet Etienne?' Paula was plainly puzzled now.

This time Etienne did the explaining.

Paula sat back and nursed her glass of wine. 'How convenient!'

'It was, wasn't it?' Mel replied with a grin and a wry little look at Etienne. 'But what did you do before you got married, Paula?'

'She was a model,' Brad said genially.

'I could still be a model if it weren't for you, Brad,' Paula pointed out. 'He doesn't like to think of his wife treading the catwalk looking sexy.'

'Would you?' Brad asked Etienne.

'I hadn't thought about it.' Etienne shrugged. 'Shall we order?'

For a time the evening went smoothly but a couple of glasses of wine later saw Paula's discontent resurface.

'Are you planning a family?' she asked of Mel.

'One day.'

'You keen for kids?' Paula transferred her attention to Etienne and bestowed upon him a caressing, all-encompassing gaze backed by the full power of her cleavage and lusciously painted, pouting lips.

'Sure,' he said easily. 'How about you two?'

'Paula has reservations,' Brad said.

'Some women are born with a maternal streak; I am not one of them,' Paula announced.

'No wonder you're bored stiff if you don't have

kids and don't have a job,' Mel said, but with genuine concern in her blue eyes. 'Although there's all sorts of charity work you could do. You know,' she turned to Brad, 'I've just had a thought. Perhaps you would consider Paula organising some charity fund-raising fashion parades?'

Etienne cleared his throat as dead silence from the other side of the table greeted this suggestion but Mel went on unaware and quite excited. 'I think that would be a great idea! Do you have a favourite charity, Paula?'

'Are you kidding?' Brad said flatly as Paula continued to regard Mel as if she'd dropped in from outer space. 'She wouldn't know one from the other and she wouldn't have the faintest idea of how to go about it!'

'It's quite simple,' Mel assured him. 'The whole trick to fund-raising is not being afraid to ask people for their time and their generosity. You may get some knock-backs but you often get some lovely surprises.'

'I suppose,' Paula said frostily, 'that's another string you have to your oh-so-efficient bow?'

'I've done a bit,' Mel agreed with a grin. 'I once organised a charity rodeo—'

'Enough!' Paula said. 'If you think I'm going to grovel around the place—'

'Well, I think Mel might be on to something,' Brad broke in. 'I think it would do you the world of good, Paula, to stop thinking about yourself to the exclusion of all else and to get out into the real world—'

He stopped abruptly as his wife emptied her wine glass over him.

*　　*　　*

'You're laughing!' Mel accused.

Etienne had extricated them from the debacle with the minimum of fuss, and once again they were on the beach, although this time in the moonlight.

'I'm laughing,' he agreed with his shoulders still shaking.

'But it was awful! I thought they were going to have an all-in brawl.'

'They may yet well do so.'

She stopped with her shoes in her hand and her expression stricken.

He turned to her, still looking wickedly amused. 'Did you have *no* idea of the mayhem you were creating, Mel?'

'I...I thought I was being helpful, that's all. I mean, it seems such an awful waste to have so much and be so discontented!'

'So you weren't,' his gaze lingered on her, 'doing it tit-for-tat?'

Mel's eyes widened. 'Certainly not—what do you mean?'

'She was sending out some rather obvious signals.'

'Oh, that.' Mel dismissed it with a wave of her hand. 'That's probably an occupational hazard I'll just have to learn to live with. No.' She paused. 'Etienne, have I been...stupid?' she asked on a lowering note.

He put his arms around her shoulders. 'You're priceless, Mel.'

'Pricelessly funny ha-ha and thick as a plank, do you mean?'

'Worth a hundred of Paula Gibson.'

Mel felt a little glow and they strolled together for a while in a companionable silence.

'Better night,' he said.

'Mmm.'

'If we weren't married, say we'd only just met, would you mind strolling in the moonlight with me—rather than walking for exercise, Mel?'

She made a little face. 'No-o. It's rather nice.'

'Then how about this?' And with the lightest touch he ran his hands up and down her arms then hooked a finger into the neckline of her top, drawing her closer so their lips were just touching and her loose tendrils of hair were blowing against his face. 'Still nice?' His lips moved against hers, his voice deep and quiet.

'Yes…'

'But?'

'If this were only the first time we'd met…' She hesitated.

'Forgive me,' he said gravely. 'I forgot for the moment what a very literal person you are.'

This time Mel flinched visibly but he went on, 'Let's speed up a bit, how about to our second date—would it be permissible then?'

'Yes…'

'Within limits, of course.'

'Etienne,' she said rather raggedly but all the same, 'I get the picture; we're going back to the beginning we missed out on.'

'Good. Nevertheless, does that mean you'd be happy to participate—on a second date?'

She hesitated then slipped her arms around his neck. And he moved his hands slowly from her armpits to her hips.

She trembled but made no attempt to move away

as he pulled her hips into his and held her there, and teased her lips open with his tongue.

One by one all her senses came alive, not only vision, taste and touch et cetera but hidden senses; the budding and flowering beneath his straying fingers of erotic areas she wasn't aware she possessed. Joyous, tantalising sensations as he caressed her throat and behind her ears, her nape, the soft skin of her armpits, her hips. Sensations that awoke in her not only her own pleasure but also a throbbing need for more.

And a need not only for more of that edgy, provoking pleasure he was bringing her with the lightest touch but also more of Etienne himself.

A desire, she identified with a spurt of shock, to be equal in this at least with the man who held all the cards of her life. Who was magnificent, clever, dynamic, always one step ahead of her and capable of just walking away from her as he'd done earlier.

A desire to conquer him with her body and claim him with her mind...

The next revelation that came to her, however, was that if anyone was being conquered, it was she. She was helpless with desire in his arms, revelling in his kiss and his hard warmth. And helpless as he gradually drew their passionate embrace to a close. His hands stopped wandering, he lifted his mouth from hers and for a long moment just held her gently against him.

She wasn't sure if she made a protesting little sound but something drew a faint smile from him.

'Let's not forget this is only our second date, Mel.'

If there was one thing she admired herself for later,

it was the way she regrouped. She took several deep breaths then pushed herself away from him, realised she'd dropped her shoes somewhere and said with a tinge of humour,

'Let's not also forget I ruined a pair of shoes on this beach only last night, Etienne!'

For a moment he didn't move a muscle as he stared narrowly into her eyes. Then his mouth relaxed and he looked around. 'Here they are. Not ruined.'

He picked them up and handed them to her. 'Want to talk about it?'

She studied her shoes and considered. 'No. But I mightn't mind if we made another...date.'

'Touché,' was his response, coming just a shade belatedly. 'However, seeing as we don't have separate homes to go to, it might be an idea if you went to bed, Mel. I'll come up later.'

'If that's supposed to make me feel foolish and virginal, Etienne—' she started to say.

But he put a finger to her lips. 'Not at all. I started this, so I, in a manner of speaking,' his dark eyes were alight with the humour of self-directed irony, 'made this bed I'm going to have to lie in tonight. I just need a drink to help me through it,' he added.

'Oh.' She bit her lip.

'And who knows, I may even find a fellow sufferer at the bar?'

'Who? You mean Brad?'

'None other. We can drown our sorrows together.'

'Etienne,' she planted her hands on her hips, 'you *did* start this but, for what it's worth, I think it's a good idea,' she said without a tremor, although that didn't nearly encompass her thoughts on the subject. 'So don't spoil it now.'

'No, ma'am.'

'And don't laugh at me either!'

'Who's laughing?'

'You are. And I *am* going to bed.' She turned away and walked up the beach.

'Just a minute, Mel.'

She stopped but didn't return to him. He'd taken his jacket off and slung it over one shoulder, and as she watched he loosened his tie. She eased her hair out of the knot it was coming out of while he apparently debated what to say.

'We haven't established when our next date will be,' he offered at last.

She tilted her chin and swirled her skirt. 'I'll think about it.'

'Now, that is…just like a woman.'

'I must be learning something!' she said wryly as she swung her arms wide, and retreated.

The next morning she was all packed and ready for their trip to Great Keppel when she came out of the bedroom to find breakfast served on the veranda. Although it had rained during the night, it was a beautiful morning with a light breeze creating a lazy pattern of ripples on the sea.

Etienne was at the table and he emerged from behind the sports pages of the paper. He hadn't shaved, he was barefoot, wearing shorts and a checked shirt. He looked, not to put too fine a point on it, moody and dishevelled.

Uh-oh, she thought as she hovered on the doorstep for a moment, what will I have to cope with today? Nor did his moody, unshaven state decrease by one iota the way he affected her. Her nerves tightened, her senses sharpened and she recalled with almost painful clarity all the responses he'd drawn from her last night.

Then she pulled herself together and joined him.

But she was not helped by the way he looked her over thoroughly, her yellow blouse and slim white trousers, her newly washed and shining hair.

'Morning, Etienne,' she said, stiffening her spine and pulling out her chair. 'How are you today?' she added and could immediately have kicked herself.

He smiled a singularly sweet smile at her, quite taking her by surprise, and raked a hand through his curly hair. 'Morning. You certainly look all bright and bushy-tailed.'

She regarded him with a faint frown. 'You don't—if you don't mind me saying so?'

'Not at all!' He reached for the coffee-pot. 'I feel,' he grimaced and rubbed the blue shadows on his jaw, 'like a horse put out to pasture.'

She frowned. 'Why?'

'I am unused, my bright and pretty wife, to being away from work for any length of time.'

'Oh! Is that all? For a moment I wondered if you might have a hangover after consorting with Brad Littleby last night.'

He laughed. 'Well, he was certainly drowning his sorrows in the bar last night but I only had one drink.'

Mel served herself some fruit and muesli. 'Did I do an awful lot of damage last night?' she asked.

'I would say the damage was already done.' Etienne sat up and took the cover off a plate of sausages, bacon and egg. 'Paula is his second wife, for whom he discarded his first wife in a fit of insanity, he now believes.'

'But why?'

He studied her wide eyes then said with irony, 'Well, you've seen her, and men in the grip of lust are not renowned for their wisdom.'

'Oh dear.'

'As you say.' He reached for the condiments. 'Would you have a solution for that?'

She stopped eating with her spoon poised. 'Why would I?'

'I was wondering if you would recommend he ditch Paula and go back to wife number one, or persevere with remodelling—' he grinned '—Paula along the lines you recommended?'

'Etienne,' she put her spoon down slowly, 'what are you trying to say? I mean, is your underlying point to do with me being a "regular little do-gooder", which seems to amuse you greatly?'

He shook some salt on his egg and some Worcestershire Sauce on his sausages.

'By the way, salt is not good for you,' she murmured.

For a moment his expression defied description.

Mel had an attack of remorse. 'Sorry, there are times when I can't resist telling people what they should and should not do. But only in their best interests.'

'Or what you perceive are their best interests.' He shot her a keen but dark little look.

'Well,' she shrugged, 'hardening of the arteries is in no one's best interests, I would have thought.'

'Eggs are one of the few things I cannot tolerate without salt.'

'Then you probably don't have anything to worry about!'

He looked at her with amazement.

'Now what?' she asked nervously.

'I don't think I've ever met anybody quite like you. Do you remember what happened on the beach last night?'

Mel coloured delicately. 'Of course. Why?'

'No reason, just checking.'

'I don't understand. Actually,' she said slowly, 'I can't work you out at all this morning. I'm not sure if you're in a good mood or a bad mood, and, if it's bad, what part of me you're objecting to.'

He stopped eating. 'It's not you I'm objecting to, it's the lack of you. In my bed, to be precise. Sadly, I'm not a patient man. But before you repeat all the rubbish I spouted last night, I will soldier on.'

For a moment she was tempted to laugh but at the same time she wasn't sure he was joking and he confused her further by finishing his breakfast with apparent enjoyment, draining his coffee-cup then standing up and telling her he would now pack for the second instalment of their so-called honeymoon.

He left her alone in her state of confusion to finish her breakfast. To make matters worse, the events on the beach last night seemed to have brought to her a permanent state of heightened awareness of Etienne from then on.

She watched him swing their bags into the boot of

the car and caught her breath as the long muscles of his back rippled. He decided to drive without consulting her and once they were closed into the car everything he did and was affected her senses. The way he flicked the gear lever brought his hands to her attention and the memories of how they'd roamed over her body.

The freshly showered scent of him in clean jeans and a navy T-shirt was almost intoxicating. Above all, or perhaps the most intimidating aspect of Etienne Hurst in a different mood, was that he seemed to catch the invisible vibes of how he was affecting her. She just knew it from the way his gaze rested on her from time to time when their arms brushed or they came into close contact.

So the contest was still on, she reflected. He may have slowed the pace of things last night but the pressure was still there, if not building up. The pressure to get her into his bed and get this marriage off the ground.

Then her mind made a quantum leap for some reason, to Brad and Paula Littleby. Why? she wondered. Because they were a prime example of lust rather than love in a relationship?

She thought about it in the car as they drove towards Rosslyn Bay, from where the ferry to Great Keppel Island left. While she may not be able to put the blame for her situation squarely on Etienne, what difference was there between their marriage and the Littlebys'?

At this point in her reflections, Etienne took a turn to the left onto a narrow side-road that led down towards the coast.

She raised her eyebrows at him.

'Something I wanted to show you,' he said, and changed down into a lower gear as the road became not only narrow and windy but also steep, with a cliff up one side and an embankment down the other.

'I hope you're not going to get my car all muddy,' she said whimsically.

He flicked her a glance. 'No. It's narrow but it's tarred all the way; it's actually a new road.'

'So, what's at the bottom?'

'Wait and see. I—' He stopped abruptly and swerved as a rock, loosened by the rain perhaps, rolled onto the road in their path—and all hell broke loose. A tall tree halfway up the cliff side of the road, that had, although they didn't know it, been precariously shored up by the rock, toppled over just as they got abreast of it.

Mel screamed as it hit the bonnet and slewed the car sideways so that it teetered on the shoulder then started to roll down the embankment.

CHAPTER NINE

'*Mel?* Are you awake?'

She swam up through a haze of pain-filled shadows and gasped as the pain was no longer shadowy but sharp and acute, all over, but mostly in her right leg.

'Etienne?' she whispered and found that her lips were dry, her mouth was dry and her eyelids seemed to be stuck together. 'Etienne? Are you all right? I think, I'm not sure, but I think I've broken my leg. *Where are you?*'

'I'm right here, Mel. I've got you in my arms—see?'

He put her hand over his and lifted them to her range of vision.

She struggled to open her eyes and their hands swam into bleary view. Then she looked upwards and his face came into focus, dark, concerned and with blood running down his cheek.

'Are we alive?' she queried.

The briefest smile twisted his lips. 'Yes, we are, very much so, but I think you may be right about your leg.'

She lifted her head and stared around. The car was resting on its roof not far away, in bushland, at the bottom of the embankment.

'Oh, my God!' She looked up towards the road.

'Yes. We were a bit lucky,' he said drily.

'My beautiful car!' The sentiment, uttered invol-

120

untarily, was nevertheless genuine, and astonished Mel. It also caused Etienne to look down at her wryly. 'Don't worry. It's insured.'

'I don't know what made me say that—are you sure you're all right? You're bleeding!'

'Just a cut. Apart from bruises and scrapes, I suspect I came off lightly. Mel,' he said gently, 'I'm going to have to make you up a splint before I move you again.'

'Were we thrown out?' she asked.

'No, but luckily you were unconscious while I got you out. Think you can handle it?'

She tried to lever herself up but gasped at the pain.

'Don't you do anything,' he warned. 'Leave it to me.'

He eased himself away from her and laid her back on the damp ground. 'Hang in there for a moment, kid, I'll have you more comfortable in a tick.'

Despite his claims of getting off lightly, Mel couldn't help noticing that he was limping as he hurried over to the car. Fortunately, the final impact must have sprung the boot, and all the suitcases were lying open in a jumble on the ground. He made several journeys, coming back with the cases, his golf clubs, a groundsheet, the car rug and the toolbox that was a standard accessory.

This was not a standard toolbox, however, he explained as he drew out a small axe and a collapsible shovel. This was a safari-level box and even came with a medical kit.

'You would never take that car on safari, would you?' she remarked with an effort. 'And why the golf clubs?'

'Maybe not but I ordered one all the same. The golf clubs? I thought they might make splints. Thing is,' he looked around, 'how to tie them on?'

'There were four pairs of brand-new pantihose in my case, my new case,' Mel said. 'Would they do?'

'Brilliant, Mrs Hurst. Just the thing. I knew that trousseau would come in handy if I bided my time,' he added with a little smile.

Twenty minutes later her leg was secure, although she was white with pain. He'd insisted on taking off her trousers, and then, with her nail scissors, had cut one leg off them and slipped it over his construction of golf clubs and pantihose as added security.

'Not the most comfortable splint but all the club heads are down round your ankle so they don't dig into you.' He knelt down beside her again. 'I just need to check you over before I move you, Mel. I did it as well as I could earlier but I'd like to be sure.'

'What for?'

'The odd cracked rib,' he said lightly but his eyes were serious and searching as his hands roamed over her, gently pressing and probing. 'I know,' he went on, 'I'm not a doctor but I insist all my staff have first-aid training—you really need it in a machine shop—then I thought I ought to lead by example. Any double vision? Or nausea?'

'I don't think so.'

'All right.' He stood up and looked around. And choosing the closest, most level piece of ground that was shaded by some scrub, he worked on it with the axe and the shovel before laying out the groundsheet and fashioning a pillow out of his clothes. Then he wedged his golf umbrella into a bush for more shade.

After that came the painful business of moving her. By the time he got her where he wanted her, she was white again and with tears streaming down her face, although no sound had escaped her lips.

'That's better,' he murmured. 'May not feel like it at the moment but it will be, I promise.' He covered her with the rug and leant over to open the first-aid kit. 'Glory be! Some extra-strong painkillers—what we need is some water.'

'I have a couple of bottles of mineral water. I took them from our bure. I also took some packets of tea, coffee and sugar, biscuits and all the toiletries from my bathroom,' she said guiltily.

'Well done—don't we all? In your bag?'

She nodded and presently she was swallowing two painkillers washed down with mineral water.

'Uh, now if I were really resourceful,' Etienne said, 'I would find a way to make you a cup of sweet, weak tea.'

She reached for his hand. 'I don't think there is a way but you've been wonderful. Is there any chance that someone will...find us?'

He looked down at her and stroked her hair. 'Sure. But it might speed things up if I could make a fire.'

Her eyes widened. 'Smoke signals—what about your mobile phone?'

He pulled a face. 'It got smashed.'

'Does anyone live around here?' she asked anxiously. 'What were you going to show me?'

'A block of ground I bought but have never developed. I was waiting for the bitumen road to go in. Uh—no one lives down here that I know of.'

'So why did they put a road in?' she asked.

'There's some talk of a fish farm being developed in the area.'

Mel was silent for a time. Silent and scared.

'Hey,' he lay down beside her, 'you've got me.'

'I know but it could be days.'

'No, it won't,' he said definitely. 'Someone will miss us. Look, why don't you close your eyes and try to sleep? If I'm not here when you wake,' she moved convulsively but he stilled her with his hands, 'I'll only be trying to get up to the road to leave a sign.'

'Could you wait until I do, if I do?'

'Of course.' He moved closer and she could smell the sweat he'd worked up and found she loved it. And the way his eyebrows were fashioned, something she'd never noticed before. His navy T-shirt was torn and dirty and the cut on his cheek ignored so that the blood had dried.

She put her fingertips to it in a butterfly touch. He caught her hand and kissed her fingers. 'You've been so brave, Mel.'

She smiled faintly. 'Why are you limping?'

'Ah, I hoped you hadn't noticed. I must have pulled a muscle in my thigh, that's all.'

The light around them was tinted green from his golf umbrella. 'We could be underwater,' she said dreamily.

'We could,' he agreed, but she missed the narrowing of his eyes as she stared upwards and he watched her.

'Two fish, maybe the first citizens of the fish farm?'

'I prefer to think of you as a lovely mermaid,' he said softly, and held his breath as her eyelids fluttered then shut.

He waited for a couple of minutes until he was sure she was asleep then eased himself away and sat up to rub his head, grit his teeth and examine his options.

He was as sure as he could be, as a layman, that she had no internal injuries and the break in her leg was a clean fracture, but he *was* only a layman despite his first-aid training. And there was the more insidious side of it to take into account—shock and possible concussion.

Up until just before she'd fallen asleep she'd seemed quite lucid, but that was not to say delayed shock wouldn't set in. That in turn meant she needed to be watched and kept warm and quiet. Therefore his best option for a speedy rescue was out of the question, he reasoned, and looked up at the road.

By his calculations they were about five kilometres away from the main road, not an impossible walk by any means but—he paused to rub the back of his leg—for someone who had done in his hamstring and was in a lot more pain than he'd let on, it would take him hours to reach the main road. Too long to leave her alone...

He looked around. There had to be some other way.

'Smoke.' Mel breathed in the definite aroma of wood smoke. She opened her eyes and looked around.

Most improbably, Etienne had a fire going and he was boiling water in a blackened old tin can, with a couple more lined up. He'd also moved two flat rocks next to the fire, one of which he was sitting on. In fact, the scrubby bushland around them had been pruned back, and in other circumstances what he'd created would have made a reasonable camp site.

He'd even cut off a slim, leafy gum shoot and was using it to wave away the bush flies.

She made a surprised sound and he got up and came over to her immediately, using one of his golf clubs as a walking stick. 'How do you feel, Mel?' He bent over her and picked up her wrist to test her pulse.

She closed her eyes again and felt pain wash through her. 'OK,' she said but swallowed hard.

'Time for some more painkillers. You've slept quite a while.'

'Have I? While you've been so busy,' she murmured. 'How did you manage it?'

'I'll tell you after you've taken these.' He helped her to sit up and she swallowed two more pills with mineral water. And he helped her to attend to a call of nature with the minimum of fuss and embarrassment, and washed her face and hands for her with a T-shirt dipped into warm water. Then he made her comfortable, making a pillow for her out of foam rubber he'd hacked out of the car seats, and wrapping her in the rug.

'Shortly,' he said, 'I'll be able to give you a cup of tea and a biscuit.' He limped back to the fire.

'You must have been a good boy scout.'

He glinted a grin across his shoulder at her. 'Never in 'em.'

'So how did you manage this?'

'I scouted around a bit and found a crevasse in the embankment with a lip of rock over it. There was a lot of dry old wood in it and these cans. I don't know if it was just coincidence or some bushwalker's cache but it all came in very handy, as you see. And, thanks to the rain, I found some rock pools.'

'But how did you light the fire?'

'You're not the only one who pinches things. I pocketed a couple of books of the resort matches—you never know when matches are going to come in handy.'

She smiled palely then frowned at the angle of the sun creeping below the golf umbrella. 'Am I wrong or is it late afternoon now?'

'You're right. It's about five o'clock.' He decanted some boiling water carefully into the smallest of the cans.

'And no one has driven past?' she queried.

'Not yet,' he said casually, and removed a tea bag from the smallest can then stirred the contents with a twig. 'But there's no chance of anyone driving past and not knowing we're here.'

'How so?'

'I climbed up to the road and planted a golf club where we rolled over, hung with a selection of our brightest clothes on it and I put the two hazard signs out of the car on either side of it. That should alert anyone going past. I have also,' he brought the can wrapped in a pair of his underpants over to her, 'been practising my smoke signals. Tea is served, ma'am!' he said deferentially and drew a couple of Cellophane-wrapped biscuit packs from his pocket.

Mel hoisted herself onto one elbow. 'Sir, you're a genius!'

'Hang on, let's see if we can sit you up for a bit.'

A few minutes later she was propped against a tree trunk.

'That's better but be careful, it's very hot,' he warned.

She blew on the liquid then drank. 'It's just what I need. Thanks.'

They shared the tea and had one biscuit each.

'OK, back to work, but listen, Mel, if you feel cold, shivery or too hot, tell me.'

'I will,' she promised, and was content to lean back and watch him try to make smoke signals.

'Hell,' he said at one stage, flapping one of his shirts over the fire, 'this is not as easy as it looks.'

She laughed softly.

'All I seem to be doing is spreading the smoke around, diffusing it in other words, the exact opposite of what I'm trying to achieve.'

'Maybe you need something bigger to flap?'

'Maybe I do.' He looked around with a frown. 'I also suspect it has something to do with the fierceness of the fire, maybe even the kindling you use; there could be all sorts of "givens" to making smoke signals.'

'I have a long dressing gown in my bag. Try that first,' she suggested.

He dug around in her bag and came out with a blue terry-cotton robe, and started to experiment with it. At first the result was much the same, or more, as they started to cough and their eyes to water in the smoke he was spreading. Then, by sheer fluke, he insisted, he began to send up round balls of smoke, twenty of them before the fire needed rebuilding.

'Success, Mrs Hurst,' he enthused and collapsed onto a rock. 'Bet you didn't think I could do it?'

'Oh, I did! I have great faith in you, Etienne! Etienne,' she pushed herself up and frowned because all of a sudden his face had tightened and he was rubbing the back of one thigh savagely, 'are you all right? Your leg—'

'Just the old hamstring. I'll be fine.'

'Why don't you take one of those painkillers?'

'I have.'

'Why don't you…relax for a bit?'

'I will. A couple more chores then I'm at your disposal, Mel.' He sent her a rather wry look and reached for his golf club.

It was dark by the time he'd finished. He'd fetched more wood, contrived to make a bed of sorts with more foam from the car seats and he'd made them a cup of coffee and doled out one more biscuit each. He'd also put more clothes on her, and socks, and donned his own jacket.

'There's nothing for it but to share a bed,' he said to her with a lurking grin, which faded as he took in her suddenly sweat-beaded brow.

'Not feeling so good, huh?' He sank down beside her.

'No. Silly of me but I'm not sure if I'm hot or cold and I keep seeing…' she stopped and swallowed '…cars rolling over and over…'

He lay down beside her and, with difficulty so as not to disturb her leg, put his arms around her. When they were comfortable, he said, 'Tell me more about Rimfire and how he got his name. Did you give it to him?'

So she told him how she'd chosen the name, from the red lights in his coat. Then he told her about the horses he'd ridden as a kid and made her laugh with some of his stories. And he told her about growing up in Gladstone and how the wharves had always fascinated him, how heavy machinery fascinated him. And how, with not much more than an engineering degree and his enthusiasm, he'd started his first marine-engineering works.

He also told her about his French mother and the trials and tribulations of her relocating from Vanuatu to Australia until he had her laughing helplessly—he could put on a perfect French accent. Although he didn't precisely say so, Mel gathered his mother and his sister, Margot, had been a lot alike, irresistible so long as you could cope with their inborn extravagance.

Once, when it was very dark and quiet, and some curlews set up their mournful calls like deserted, sobbing children, he started to sing to her in a soft baritone.

As she lay nestled against him, despite the pain she was in, her delayed shock began to wane, her fear that they wouldn't be rescued ebbed—and she thought she could listen to him forever.

They slept on and off through the night. He got up several times to feed the fire, and give her more painkillers and, when he came back, warmed his cold hands on her body.

Once, he slept while she stayed awake. One of his arms was lying across her body and her head was resting in the curve of his shoulder. And it came to her that, after this, she could never not care about Etienne Hurst.

Was it worse, though? she wondered. Could she ever be as aware of another man as she was of him? Aware now of not only his strength but also the experience of his gentleness?

He had handled her and helped through this accident so well, she thought. Not even a broken leg could have taken the embarrassment out of some of the functions he'd helped her with today, so, without her realising it, he'd got her to trust him.

And even as sore and throbbing with pain as she was, lying against him, feeling his warmth and bulk, breathing in the pure man of him was not only reassuring but also rather lovely.

Maybe I've been a bit of a fool, she thought. Or maybe I needed something like this to show me a side of Etienne I could believe in and relate to?

'Mel?' he said sleepily. 'How's it going?'

She nestled closer to him. 'I was just thinking, that's all.'

'Good thoughts?' He moved carefully and began to stroke her hair.

'Pretty good,' she said drowsily.

'That's my girl.'

But at first light she was in serious pain again, Etienne could see, although she was trying to hide it. And he'd just about decided he would have to try to reach the main road, when he heard the sound of a motor.

He shot up from the water he was boiling, swore as his leg ached abominably, and a tall, heavy-set man accompanied by two huge dogs scrambled down the embankment.

'Holy cow!' this individual expostulated. 'How d'you survive that?' He gestured to the car with his hat.

'By the skin of our teeth, mate,' Etienne said.

'Thank heavens you've come; I didn't think it likely many people would drive down this road.'

'I don't usually but I was yarning with my neighbour last night and he mentioned seeing some funny smoke signals down here yesterday—thought he was having me on, he drinks a fair bit, but when I woke up this morning I decided I'd better investigate. She all right?' He looked across at Mel.

'No. She's broken her leg, we need help.'

'Right—' The man stiffened. 'Mel, is that you?'

Mel raised her head. 'Jim Dalton!' she said weakly. 'How wonderful to see you!'

'You just hang in there, honey,' Jim Dalton said intensely as he bent over Mel. 'I've got a CB radio in my truck! I'll get you out of here.' He turned away and literally threw himself at the embankment.

Things moved fast after that. A rescue helicopter was called in with a doctor on board. In the moments before Mel was winched aboard on a stretcher, Etienne explained that he wouldn't be able to go with her—there wasn't room for him.

And for only the second time since the accident, she shed some tears and clung to him.

'You'll be fine,' he murmured and smoothed her hair. 'You're the bravest girl in the world!' He smiled down into her eyes.

'You're not too bad yourself,' she replied out of a clogged throat. 'Thanks for everything!'

His hand tightened on hers then he let her go.

'Where d'you learn to make them smoke signals?' Jim Dalton asked.

Etienne didn't take his eyes off the stretcher until

it was safely aboard the hovering helicopter and it had swooped away, relieving them of the whirlwind downdraught of leaves and twigs. 'I think I might have some Apache blood in me,' he said seriously and sat down rather suddenly on his rock.

'Here.'

He looked up to see he was being offered a hip flask.

'Brandy?' he hazarded.

'Of a sort; my own home brew.'

'Jim, you're a lifesaver.' Etienne took the flask and swallowed gratefully. 'Brrr…' He wiped his eyes and cleared his throat. 'Damn fine brew, mate!'

'Yep! How'd it happen?'

Etienne explained briefly.

Jim scratched his head. 'The rain must have loosened the rock and the tree. Sometimes takes a while for new works to bed down. Oh, well, there's a flatbed trailer and a crane on the way.'

'Thanks. By the way, I'm Etienne Hurst.' They shook hands. 'How do you come to know Mel, Jim?'

'Used to do some work on the property for her father. So. You're the guy who married her?' Jim sat down on a rock and started to roll himself a homemade cigarette. At the same time as his fingers expertly completed the task, he subjected Etienne to a rather unnerving gaze from his far-seeing blue eyes.

'Yes.'

'Came as a bit of a surprise,' Jim offered thoughtfully, lighting up with a battered old Zippo lighter.

'I suppose it did.'

Jim squinted through the smoke and waved some

flies away. 'Now, there's some people that think Mel can be difficult. I ain't one of them.'

'Oh?'

'Yep. She really cares about things. She did something for my wife once no one else would have thought of doing. They all stood by and were afraid to meddle. Not Mel. That's why I'm proud and it's a pleasure to know her.'

'Jim,' Etienne frowned, 'are you trying to tell me something?'

Jim crossed his legs and studied the tip of his cigarette. 'All sorts of rumours flying around about your wedding, mate.'

'I can imagine.'

'In fact a lot of people are saying she's the last girl they thought you'd marry.'

'Jim,' Etienne smiled rather grimly, 'it has nothing to do with anyone but Mel and myself.'

'Sure.' Jim waved a hand negligently. 'But you'd be surprised how many people out there care about Mel Ethridge and wouldn't like to see her get hurt. OK. I've said my piece.' He cocked his head. 'Sounds like some action arriving. I'll go up and direct the traffic.'

Etienne sat quite still as once more Jim laboured up the embankment. Then he picked up the nearest thing to hand, which happened to be one of the flimsy nightgowns, now torn and muddy, that Mel had refused to wear, and he stared at it with his mouth set and a muscle flickering in his jaw.

CHAPTER TEN

FOUR days later Mel deployed her crutches and teetered on the front steps of the Gladstone Base Hospital.

Getting the hang of not only the crutches but also the cast on her leg had taken some doing. She'd spent the last days in hospital after being rescued, while X-rays had been taken and consultations held as to whether she would need to have the bone pinned. Thankfully it had been deemed not necessary so she'd been saved an operation, and, due to an impressive array of bruises as well as stiffness and feeling as weak as a kitten, she hadn't minded her days in bed.

She'd had plenty of visitors, including the one she wanted most, Etienne. He'd come twice a day and the camaraderie of their time at the bottom of the embankment was the same. But they'd rarely been alone.

Now he was taking her home—in a brand-new four-wheel-drive vehicle.

She stood poised on the hospital steps and blinked at the midnight-blue vehicle with its distinctive number plate—MEL 1.

'Is this what I think it is?' she asked.

'More appropriate than the last car I gave you, don't you agree?' he murmured.

'But…but…' she stammered.

'As good a work horse as a ute but more comfortable,' he added.

She subsided. 'I guess I have as little say in this as I had in the other—thank you.'

'My pleasure, ma'am. Unfortunately, your other beautiful car was beyond redemption.'

'That's sad but you're right, this is more practical.' She eyed the steep step. 'How do I get into it, though?'

'Hold on to me, prop your crutches here and,' he picked her up and deposited her carefully in the front seat, 'like so—for the time being.'

'I can't wait to get home,' she told him as they drove out of Gladstone, cushioned in sheepskin covers, breathing in new leather and from the lofty vantage point of the Range Rover.

'I thought you were pretty comfortable in hospital?'

'I was but now I'm out—by the way,' she turned to him, 'how's *your* leg?'

'Improving. I've had a bit of physio. Mel, I've been meaning to ask you something—what did you do for Jim Dalton's wife?'

Mel looked surprised. 'Jim mentioned it?'

'He did. Plus his boundless admiration for you.'

She coloured faintly. 'Nothing very much.'

'He seemed to think it was.'

'She, well, she used to work for us. Once a week she'd come in and do the heavy cleaning for Mrs B. I guess at this time she was about eighteen, still living at home with her widowed father.

'Anyway, one day I noticed that she had a black eye, although she'd tried to cover it up. And, when I thought about it, I realised she often had bruises so I asked her about it. She would only say she'd been clumsy. But I decided to ask around. The general consensus was that her father was an alcoholic who regularly beat her up and wouldn't let her leave home.'

'So you decided to intervene?'

'Yes.'

'How?'

'Well, I went out of my way to get to know Sophie better and to try to get her to trust me. Then one day she came to work in an awful state and she broke down and told me what was going on at home and how all she wanted to do was run away but she didn't have anywhere to go. So I told her to stay with us for as long as she wanted to.' Mel broke off.

'Go on.'

'And when her father roared up one day to claim her, I warned him off with a shotgun.'

'What else?' he marvelled. 'Where was *your* father?'

'Away at the time.' Mel looked rueful. 'He always used to say, when the cat's away the mice will play! And not always nicely either. He was furious with me, not because something didn't need to be done but because I'd endangered us all. I tried to point out that I couldn't help the *timing* of it but he wasn't impressed. Anyway, that's when Jim took a hand, thankfully.'

'How so?'

'He'd been admiring Sophie from afar. He'd seen her often while he'd been working at Raspberry Hill but he hadn't known her background. And a combination of shyness on both their parts plus poor Sophie's lack of self-esteem hadn't see them do anything more than look. But after the drama of having to warn Sophie's dad off with a gun, Jim came around breathing fire and he took Sophie under his wing and married her! That was two years ago and they have a baby now and are really happy.'

'And her father?' Etienne looked at her questioningly.

'Well, you don't argue with Jim Dalton.' Mel looked across at Etienne with a grin and was surprised to receive a glance full of ironic agreement in return. 'Uh—anyway, we've persuaded him to take the cure.'

'Alcoholics Anonymous?'

'Yes, but I think it's still a long, hard road for him and I don't know if he'll ever make it.'

'You're a bleeding marvel, Mrs Hurst,' Etienne said softly.

'The way my father put it at the time was—once again I'd rushed in where angels feared to tread.'

Etienne grinned. 'I may have shared his sentiments—at the time.'

They drove in silence for a while then she said, 'Another thing I've been meaning to ask you—have you been living at home while I've been in hospital?'

'Yes. I've officially moved in. Just as well as it turns out.' He swung the wheel and they entered the long drive to Raspberry Hill.

Mel looked out over the green paddocks pasturing fat cattle on one side of the drive, and the orderly dark green rows of pineapples on the other with deep affection. Then she registered what he'd said.

'How so?' she asked with some misgiving. 'Or, let me guess—Tosh?'

'How did you know?'

'He's been looking particularly innocent the last

two days. I tried to tell myself it was my imagination—OK, what's he done now?' she enquired with resignation.

Etienne paused. 'I struck a deal with him. Part of it was that you needn't be told.'

They were driving past the glorious purple tibouchinas that lined the last part of the drive. 'But you've more or less told me,' she objected.

'It slipped out, I'm afraid. But rest assured, he's duly repentant and no further action is required.'

'How,' Mel smiled at the lillypilly trees standing sentinel as the drive opened into the gravel circle in front of the house—she loved the way their leaves turned bright pink in spring as they were now, 'did you get him to be repentant?'

Again Etienne paused. 'He might take me more seriously than he does you, Mel.'

'You didn't,' she turned to him urgently, 'you didn't—'

'I didn't use corporal punishment if that's what you're worried about,' he broke in drily.

'Sorry. Oh.' The car rolled to a stop and Mrs Bedwell emerged onto the veranda, followed by the three boys. 'Whatever Tosh did, it's good to be home!'

He switched off and turned to her. 'Promise me one thing?'

She raised an eyebrow at him.

'You'll take it easy.'

Her hands moved in her lap as the desire gripped her to run her fingers through his hair and press herself into his arms. 'Yes, I will,' she said huskily, and held her breath.

'Good girl.' If he'd noticed the sort of melting process she was going through, he gave no sign as he swung himself out of the driver's seat and came round to lift her out of the car. The boys and Mrs Bedwell surrounded them, and even Batman came out to greet her rather than Etienne.

That night, though, she wasn't so sure about the pure pleasure of being home.

She tried to tell herself it was her imagination; either that or concern for her was responsible for a change in Etienne. Not that there was much of a change, she thought. The same friendliness, there was genuine concern, but a closer closeness? The kind they'd experienced before being rescued, the kind she'd found herself desperately wanting to continue— had that gone?

She looked around her new bedroom. Mary Lees and Mrs Bedwell had either taken it upon themselves or followed Etienne's orders to convert a guest bedroom into the new master bedroom. With the result that she lay in a new king-size bed—in solitary state.

A night-light revealed a pleasant room. Her own lovely cedar dressing table and chest of drawers, inherited from her mother, and the colour scheme was chalk-blue and ivory. The bedroom opened onto a side veranda below which grew several orange trees, and when they were flowering the lovely scent of orange blossom wafted into this side of the house.

Several vases with some of the beautiful flowers she'd received in hospital were set about, roses, carnations, liliums. So there was nothing she could take issue with about her new bedroom—except Etienne's absence.

Could she really take exception to that? she wondered. He'd explained that for the time being he would use the smaller bedroom on the other side of an inter-leading bathroom, so she could get as much rest as possible.

It had even made sense at the time. Not long after dinner, she'd been white with tiredness and the unfamiliar business of coping with crutches as well as the pain of a broken leg, and more than happy to go to bed.

She'd even been happy to be tucked in by him and administered the light sedative the hospital had supplied, after Mrs Bedwell had helped her to change. She'd murmured goodnight to him at the same time as she'd had difficulty keeping her eyes open.

But once he'd gone and before the sleeping pill took effect, she'd felt curiously awake and alert and particularly receptive to every nuance on the air.

Now, awake again in the early hours, she recalled that strange heightening of her perception and the lonely feeling it had brought to her. *Was* it her imagination or had she read more into their time together at the bottom of the embankment than had existed?

She moved restlessly and tried to ease her leg into a more comfortable position. If that was so, and perhaps possible because of the heightened tension, was she feeling let down now because she'd expected more from Etienne?

Am I looking down the barrel of having my feelings for him crystallise into knowing I've fallen in love with him, whereas he is still only locked into a marriage of convenience? she mused painfully.

Or am I still too sore and disorientated by the accident to be judging anything accurately?

Three weeks later Mary Lees came to lunch, a working lunch.

Much more proficient on her crutches, Mel greeted her and led her to a table set on the veranda.

'How lovely,' Mary enthused. 'And you're looking so much better, Mel!' Mary had visited her in hospital.

'Thanks.' Mel balanced on one leg and pulled out a chair for her guest. 'It took me a while to get used to these, though!' She sank down into her own chair and laid her crutches against the railing.

'How long do you have to be in the cast?'

Mel grimaced. 'Another two months. But I've decided to put this period to good use. That's why I need your help, Mary.'

'I'm only too delighted to help.' Mary paused and hesitated. 'You mentioned on the phone that you expected to start entertaining for Etienne but honestly, Mel, I could do it while you're,' she gestured to the crutches, 'like this. I've done quite a few business lunches and dinners for him.'

Mel reached for the open bottle of wine. 'Would you like a glass?'

'Thank you!'

Mel poured two glasses. 'The thing is, Mary, I feel a bit guilty because I'm probably doing you out of some business, but I would really like to do this myself only I don't have much experience. So I need to acquire some of your expertise.'

'If you want my opinion,' Mrs Bedwell stalked

onto the veranda with two bowls of summer soup, pale green and delicately swirled with cream, 'you're best off just being yourself, Mel, and leaving the rest up to me!' She retreated indoors on that note.

Mel eyed her stiff back over the rim of her glass then turned to Mary to encounter a humorous look.

'I see how the land lies,' Mary said softly, 'but she could be right.'

Mel shrugged. 'She often is but I'm determined to do this *well*. You see,' she confessed, 'I may have a reputation for rushing in where angels fear to tread but the thought of entertaining a whole lot of people I don't know gives me the screaming heebie-jeebies.'

Mary laughed with genuine amusement but she sobered as they tucked into their soup. 'I don't know if I can give you that…expertise, for want of a better word, Mel. Some people just seem to have it, others don't.'

'I know what you mean.' Mel smiled ruefully. 'My stepmother had it in abundance, but there must be some things I can learn.'

Something alert entered Mary's brown gaze.

'Take clothes, for example,' Mel continued. 'I've never given them much thought. And, sadly, the lovely ones you chose for my trousseau mostly got ruined in the accident. Where did you get them? I've never seen their likes around here. Well, other than on my stepmother.'

'Brisbane,' Mary said succinctly.

'And…and,' Mel finished her soup and pushed her plate away, 'table decorations. Both Mrs Bedwell and I are quite happy to put a bunch of flowers on the table—that's the height of our artistic creativity—but

Margot went to infinite pains to make her tables exquisite, or humorous, or jungly or oriental—something, so they became a talking point.'

'I never met Etienne's sister,' Mary confided, 'but on the clothes front I have quite a few country clients I shop for in Brisbane.'

'You must spend a lot of time travelling!'

'I do.' Mary smiled. Then she said thoughtfully, 'Mel, do you have anything in particular coming up?'

'Yes, in three weeks; Etienne has some Malaysian visitors arriving. His shipping agency handles their bulk coal carriers when they come into Gladstone. Two men and their wives—it's a part-business, part-holiday trip, I gather. I'd like to give a dinner for them.'

Mrs Bedwell arrived to deliver grilled Atlantic salmon garnished with dill and accompanied by fried rice. 'Please join us, Mrs B,' Mel added.

For a moment Mrs Bedwell looked stubborn, then she shrugged and drew up a chair. 'I've had mine so I'll just rest my legs for a bit.'

'Why don't you have a glass of wine?'

Mrs Bedwell pursed her lips then went away to get a glass.

'You are a marvellous cook,' Mary Lees said to her when she returned. 'This is delicious.'

'Thank you.' Mrs Bedwell looked regal. 'That's why I wonder about Mel needing any other assistance to entertain, if you'll pardon me speaking plainly.'

Mary sipped her wine as she masked her need to choose her words with care. 'If I were doing this dinner, here's how I'd proceed—how many people does your main dining-room table hold comfortably?'

'Twelve,' Mrs Bedwell supplied promptly.

'Right. So with you and Etienne plus the Malaysian guests, that gives us six—I would look for six more guests. Now, I happen to know that Etienne generally likes to have his second-in-command, who has a delightful wife, in on even quasi-business affairs. That leaves four more people to find.'

Mel rubbed her chin. 'Can't think of one.'

'How about the mayor and his wife?' Mary suggested. 'The business side of this visit obviously involves the port of Gladstone, so they would be very appropriate. Or, if they're unavailable, the harbour master.'

Mel stared at her with her eyes widening. 'I see what you mean—mind you, since I tried to ride my horse into the council chamber—'

'Told you not to do that!' Mrs Bedwell put in severely. 'But they won't hold that against you any more.'

'Why not?'

'Not now you're Mrs Etienne Hurst, Mel, rest assured,' Mrs Bedwell said complacently.

'Oh. I hadn't thought of that.'

'You never do,' her housekeeper remarked with slightly exasperated affection, and turned back to Mary Lees. 'That leaves us two short.'

'Well,' Mary dabbed her lips, 'for the last two I'd look for people with something in common with the visitors.'

Mrs Bedwell screwed up her face. 'Don't know any shipping magnates or people of Malay origin, do you, Mel?'

'As a matter of fact, I do,' Mel said slowly. 'Mary,

you're a genius! The president of the RSPCA has a Malaysian wife and they're both lovely people!'

'There you go!' Mary smiled warmly at her.

But Mel subsided abruptly. 'That doesn't mean to say once I've got them all together round a dining table that I'll be able to,' she gestured, 'conjure up a successful dinner party.'

'Several points,' Mary said. 'You have Etienne so you won't be flying solo and he's very good at it. Second, don't be afraid of the mundane—most people love talking about their kids or their grandkids, where they're going on holiday, where they buy their meat, what football team they follow, who's going to win the Melbourne Cup—and once you establish a rapport on a common level, things seem to open up of their own accord.'

'True,' Mrs Bedwell agreed, and looked at Mary with new respect. 'Of course, it also helps to remember they're guests, and they might not enjoy the subjects of land-mines, abattoirs, injustices to asylum-seekers, child labour and so on over their meal.'

Mel grinned fleetingly. 'Point taken, Mrs B, but I can't always help myself.'

'So long as you don't actually lecture people,' Mary put in with a grin. 'The thing is, once you've established with your guests that you're really interested in them you can talk about what you like.'

'OK. Well, I feel a lot better about it now. But about table decorations?' She raised her eyebrows at Mary.

'I...' Mary paused. 'No slight intended towards your stepmother, Mel, but I think candles and flowers are enough for a dinner table, especially if you have nice china, linen, silver and crystal. I don't like over-crowded tables, and men, particularly, find them a hazard.'

'We have more china and stuff than you could poke a stick at,' Mrs Bedwell said rather drily and with a glance at Mel. 'We have a brand-new Wedgwood service not even out of its packing. And Mel's rather good at making unusual arrangements out of leaves and flowering natives like callistemon and lillypilly—she really does them nicely.'

'There you go. Uh—seating plans. Some numbers like eight and twelve don't work out with the host and hostess at either end opposite each other, they won't go man, woman, man, woman, in other words, so you need to have either two men or two women at the head and the foot—'

'That's why Mrs Ethridge ordered a new round table,' Mrs Bedwell remarked.

'Good,' Mary approved, 'solves that problem. Otherwise, separate husbands and wives, don't try to establish any pecking order for this kind of dinner, and if, during the preliminaries, you see someone who is particularly shy, give them to yourself or Etienne.'

'Right.' Mel pondered briefly. 'Should I send out formal invitations?'

'I would,' Mary said, 'but I'd also check the guest list with Etienne beforehand.'

Mel nodded. 'That leaves clothes.' She looked down at the cast on her leg. 'There's no way I can hide this but a long skirt might make it less obvious.'

'There's a young designer in Brisbane I've recently stumbled on,' Mary said slowly. 'Her ideas are fresh and chic. I'm wondering if it wouldn't be a thought to get her to design a wardrobe for you? That way you'd have some input but not the hassle of shopping. After all, your choice of wedding dress was stunning.'

'Maybe, but I don't think it's necessary to get a whole wardrobe and—'

'I think it's a brilliant idea,' Mrs Bedwell interrupted.

'But I don't really want to go to Brisbane—'

'She would be more than happy to come up here for a day.' Mary interrupted Mel this time.

'Just for me? I doubt it,' Mel objected.

'She may not have for Mel Ethridge, but Mrs Etienne Hurst is another matter,' Mrs Bedwell said shrewdly.

'Precisely,' Mary concurred.

I might believe this confidence everyone has in the powers of Mrs Etienne Hurst if I really was the lady, Mel thought a shade grimly, then shrugged.

'Perhaps you're right. It would solve the clothes problem. Is she terribly expensive, though?'

'I feel she's quite reasonable. And really,' Mary looked at Mrs Bedwell, her new ally, 'good clothes are an investment and a saving.'

Mrs Bedwell nodded sagely, causing Mel to smile inwardly because Mrs Bedwell's approach to dressing was an arbitrary affair at best, and at worst she looked like a tall, colourful rag bag.

'Well,' Mary looked from Mel to Mrs Bedwell, 'that wasn't so difficult, was it?'

'A piece of cake!' Mrs Bedwell rose. 'Talking of that, I'll get dessert and coffee.'

*   *   *

That evening Mel described her day to Etienne after dinner.

They were in the den, the boys were quiet, supposedly doing their homework, and a light drizzle was falling.

'Difficult day?' she asked, when he stretched and lay back in his chair with a sigh. He'd changed into a pair of combat trousers and a striped T-shirt.

'On the shipping front, slightly tricky, that's all. One of the coal loaders needed maintenance, which meant rescheduling the two bulk carriers we had waiting to come in, as well as establishing their load barriers and balances.'

'What does that mean?'

'Well, basically, you have to load a ship as evenly as possible. In untechnical terms hulls have stress areas, so, in the case of one of them, we could have brought them in and loaded one hold to capacity with the loader that was working, but consultation with the Taiwanese captain, who didn't speak much English, revealed his ship's stress level wouldn't allow it. That meant a delay and delays cost money.'

'I get you! That's interesting.'

'You should come down to the agency office one day, Mel. Justin's already paid us a few visits.'

'And just think how impressive it would be if I could discuss hull stress levels with your Malaysian visitors,' she said with a grin.

He sat up. 'About them, Mel, I've been thinking.'

'Think no more, Etienne, it's all taken care of!'

He cocked an eyebrow at her.

So she told him about her lunch with Mary Lees and the consequences thereof. 'Here's the proposed guest list, which I was told I should clear with you first.'

He got up, took a piece of paper from her and ran his eye down the list. 'The mayor!' He looked at her with palpable amusement. 'That's brave of you, Mel.'

'I'm reliably informed, Etienne, that as your wife I can—get away with blue murder!' She paused and grimaced. 'I'm just a little worried that the other thing I've done today falls into that category,' she confessed, and told him about the dress designer due to descend on her shortly.

'What's wrong with that?'

'It seems…rather extravagant. I mean, it's all very well for *you* to spend your money on me to shore up your pride or whatever but…but both Mary and Mrs Bedwell badgered me into it, if you really want to know.'

He looked down at her. 'I'm with Mary and Mrs Bedwell. However, I don't think this dinner party is such a good idea.'

All set to make some pithy retort, Mel stopped with her mouth open. She closed it and said instead, 'Why not?'

'You have a broken leg,' he pointed out. 'The more rest you give it, the more chance it has of healing cleanly and well.'

'I can do just about all of it sitting down. It's not as if I'm doing the cooking or the shopping.'

He pulled up a stool and sat down in front of her. 'You promised me you would take things easy, Mel.'

She swallowed and it flashed through her mind to tell him that was before she'd divined he was having second thoughts about marrying her. Of course, the irrationality of it occurred to her simultaneously so she said nothing. 'Mel?'

'Etienne, I want to do it,' she said after a long pause. 'For a few reasons, I guess. Sitting still doesn't come easily to me so at least this is something I can plan and work towards without too much physical effort.' She hesitated.

'And?'

She glanced across at him then tapped her cast. 'I feel I'd like to repay you in some way for all the things you've done for me. I guess I thought being a *useful* wife, if nothing else, would be a way to do that.'

His dark gaze roamed over her bright hair and her troubled eyes.

'Of course,' she continued in a way that she could only think of later as being her own devil's advocate, 'it's impossible to be much of a wife with a broken leg, I do see that, and I thank you for your consideration in the matter, but—' She stopped as he smiled faintly.

'Well, you know what I mean!' She looked at him with a flash of exasperation.

'Naturally.'

'Then why don't you contribute something useful to this conversation rather than letting me plough on and make a fool of myself?' This time the exasperation was touched with annoyance.

'You're not making a fool of yourself, Mel. You're very sweet.' He paused and his eyes narrowed. 'All right,' he said as if coming to a sudden decision, 'you may hold this dinner party. On one condition. If I think you're doing too much I reserve the right to pull the plug.'

Their gazes clashed. Say something more, she begged him in her mind. Or, at least put your arms around me—OK, perhaps it's not possible to make love to someone with a broken leg but...

She closed her eyes briefly then looked away. 'Thank you. I'll try and make it a memorable evening.'

'Hi, guys!' Justin wandered into the room. 'Not interrupting anything, am I?'

'Not at all.' Etienne got up and returned to his chair.

'Not much of a night.' Justin wandered over to the French doors. 'I was going up to play tennis with Freddie Calder but it's been called off.'

'They have lights on their court?' Etienne asked.

'They have everything that opens and shuts. All my life I've been living in Freddie Calder's shadow.'

'What's that mean?' Tosh wandered in with Batman under his arm.

'It means Justin is feeling sorry for himself about all the things Freddie has that he doesn't.' Ewan came in and over to Mel. 'What do you think of this?'

She took the chalk drawing he held out to her, and started to laugh. 'Ewan! That's not fair!'

'Why?'

It was a remarkably accurate interpretation of Batman dressed up as the devil.

'He's improving. I think.' She glanced over to where Tosh was playing on the carpet with the dog.

'He's getting worse if you ask me! He did something unmentionable this morning.' Ewan looked disgusted.

Tosh, alerted to the trend of the conversation, sat up as Justin took the etching and started to laugh. 'Let me see!'

'Sure!' Justin handed over the piece of paper. 'Why don't you stick it up over your bed?'

But Tosh tore the paper up, and, scooping up his dog, retreated in a high dudgeon.

'What do they say about great artists not being recognised in their own homes?' Justin remarked and cuffed Ewan jovially.

'Cut it out!' Ewan objected.

'Do I detect a note of boredom in the air?' Etienne drawled.

'You do, mate,' Justin replied. 'Any suggestions?'

'Yep.' Etienne stood up. 'It's occurred to me you boys are under-worked and over-paid—' Ewan and Justin groaned in unison but Etienne ignored them '—so I thought you might like to help me mark out the golf putting green I had in mind.'

'In the rain?' Mel put in.

'That's not rain.' Etienne smiled at her. 'Let's go, fellas. Get Tosh too.'

Mel took herself to bed and tried to read before they came back in. But she couldn't concentrate on her book because of the circles of her mind.

For the most part, Etienne had transposed his life seamlessly into their lives. Yet a sense of permanence was lacking, she thought. Because, as he'd told her, he'd maintained his apartment in Gladstone and sometimes, when he worked very late, he stayed there rather than driving out to Raspberry Hill?

It made sense. Not that she knew a great deal about Hurst Engineering & Shipping yet but she was learning that, as such a high-profile and successful businessman, he had a lot of calls on his time. But *did* it make sense in the context of the present state of their marriage? she wondered forlornly.

Which was to say, since he'd ended all forms of closeness between them, physical and emotional other than being like a good friend, did he need other women? For which his apartment was ideal?

And why was he in two minds about her giving this dinner party? Solely because of her leg or—because once she was fully recovered, he didn't intend to continue the marriage and therefore presenting her as his wife was undiplomatic to say the least?

In all other respects he'd been brilliant, though. The boys liked and admired him and their lives were running smoothly again, thanks to his organisation. The farm was running smoothly…

She broke off her thoughts as she heard the four of them return, in audibly good spirits.

Then, as the house grew quiet, Etienne knocked at her door and padded into the room in his socks and clean clothes. His hair was damp and there was a glow of vitality about him.

'It went well?' she suggested, putting a bookmark in her book.

'Yes. They're going to do all the work and we plan to include a cricket practice net.'

'Inspired thinking,' she murmured.

He stood at the bottom of the bed. 'Keeping them

busy is half the battle, I suspect. How are you feeling? Do you still need something to help you sleep at night?'

'No. I stopped them a while back.'

'No—' his eyes searched hers '—nightmares?'

She hesitated too long then couldn't lie.

He sat down on the side of the bed. 'Tell me.'

'Just the odd one.'

'Cars rolling down embankments?'

She nodded.

'Anything else? Mel?' He said her name in a way that indicated he expected an answer.

'That's about it,' she murmured but couldn't prevent some faint colour stealing into her cheeks.

'You're lying,' he said softly.

She lay against the pillows in her Snoopy pyjamas and thought of telling him that the one sure way to stop her nightmares, of cars and waking up drenched in sweat because she'd dreamt she was at the bottom of the embankment on her own, would be to lie down beside her and hold her as she slept.

Why wouldn't he know it, though? Why wouldn't he do it unless...?

She shrugged, a slight movement of her slim shoulders. 'Sometimes I'm not sure what wakes me up. But I guess it'll all fade. It is,' she assured him.

His gaze wandered down to the curve of her breasts beneath the cotton of her top. Then he said abruptly, 'Mel, not that I would ever wish it to happen the way it did, but perhaps this has given us the breathing space we needed.'

Her eyes widened.

He looked away briefly. 'The time we need to grow

together and get to know each other better. I even thought that was something you would approve of.'

She swallowed.

'You gave me some quite clear indications that's what you thought before the accident,' he said.

'I guess you're right,' she said at last.

'Then why are you unhappy?' he asked.

'I don't know,' she temporised. 'Well, it's not easy being—one-legged. I can't even go out and look for a horse for you, I can't do anything for Rimfire. I suppose I feel useless, bored and...all those things over and over again.'

He sat back. 'Two months is not a lifetime.'

She shrugged. 'I know. Really, I'm fine! They did warn me I could get post-accident blues, this must be a blue patch, that's all.'

'Mel,' Tosh burst into the bedroom without knocking, 'Ewan can't breathe!'

CHAPTER ELEVEN

AN HOUR later, Ewan was breathing on his own, although looking wan and exhausted.

Mel wrapped the oxygen mask up and looked across at Etienne. 'I'll sleep here tonight, in Tosh's bed,' she said calmly and casually.

'Wow! Does that mean I can sleep in your bed, Mel?' Tosh asked.

'No, it does not! You can use the spare bed in Justin's room.'

'Wise thinking,' Ewan murmured and closed his eyes. 'It's about time Justin had to share the damn dog.'

'He must be feeling better to be wishing Batman on me,' Justin declared ruefully.

And Etienne felt real affection tug at him for this family he'd taken over. His immediate instinct had been to call an ambulance despite his first-aid training. But Mel had coped with serenity and confidence, which, of course, had played a crucial role in helping Ewan through the attack. And Justin and Tosh had been discreetly supportive of their sister and sick brother.

'You don't need to sleep here, Mellie,' Ewan said drowsily. 'I'm OK now.'

Etienne stirred. 'May I make a suggestion? How about I share your room, Ewan?'

Mel went to speak but Etienne shook his head at

her barely perceptibly, and went on, 'That way we can all get a good night's rest.'

'OK. Suits me!' Ewan turned over.

Mel was back in her bed where Etienne had carried her and a few minutes later he came back with a cup of cocoa for her.

'You did well, Mel,' he said as he put it down on her bedside table. 'So well.'

'Thank you, but I've had a bit of practice and I really wouldn't have minded sleeping with Ewan.'

'I watched you so I know what to do, and it has to be easier for someone who doesn't have a—'

'A broken leg,' she supplied.

'Yep!' He grinned. 'Don't want to harp on it but someone needs to.'

'So long as Ewan knows you can cope—'

'Hey—stop worrying,' he said. 'I won't let him, or you, down.'

Mel drank some cocoa then yawned widely behind her fingers.

'Now, that is a good sign, as I know from previous experience,' he said softly and took the cup from her, tucked her in and dropped a light kiss on her hair. 'Sleep well, princess.'

She fell asleep oddly reassured.

Three weeks later she wasn't so sure again.

The day of the dinner party was upon her and her nerves were showing. It had been an uneventful three weeks during which she'd held good to her promise to give her leg as good a chance of healing as possible—apart from two instances.

Once, Etienne had caught her hopping down to the stables on her crutches, and told her she was a bloody idiot.

'Why the hell you knocked back a wheelchair, I'll never know,' he added, his eyes grim and his mouth setting hard.

'I'd prefer it if you didn't swear at me, Etienne,' she responded, 'and for your information they told me I didn't need one.'

'Well, I know you a damn sight better than they do,' he said deliberately. 'Couldn't you have asked for someone to bring Rimfire up to the house so you could say hello?'

'It takes up enough of Mrs Bedwell's time having to feed him as it is. I don't like to ask her—'

'Of course, this is the horse that eats men,' he marvelled. 'Only you could have one of those, Mel!'

'And only you could be so annoying, Etienne,' she shot back. 'It's not my fault he hates men! Besides, I'm worried about him. He's not getting enough exercise.'

'Then put him in a paddock for the time being. Or ask Mrs B to do it. It'll save her having to feed him.'

'Well, I thought of that but he could be lonely, at least in the stable he's got Tosh's pony to talk to.'

'Mel,' Etienne said dangerously, 'do you want to hold this dinner party or not?'

'Of course I want to hold it but it's ridiculous for *you* to hold it over my head like this as if I were a two-year-old!'

'No, it's not, so the horse goes into a paddock, along with the damn pony if necessary, and you stop trying to sneak down to the stables. Understood?'

Since she had her hands full of crutches and a cast on her leg, her preferred options of slapping his face then stalking away were unattainable.

'And before you bust a gut, Mel,' he advised softly as his gaze travelled over her scarlet face and furious eyes, 'I must tell you I regard you as particularly sane and admirable in just about every respect other than this.'

Shock caused her to teeter on her crutches briefly. 'You do?'

'Yes, I do. You were marvellous at the bottom of the embankment when you must have been in terrible pain. You were terrific with Ewan the other night and a whole lot more besides, so don't disappoint me over this.'

'Then why…?' She stopped and bit her lip.

'Why?' he repeated.

'It doesn't matter. OK, Rimfire can go into the paddock and I'll go back to the house.' She turned and started to hop away.

'Stay here. Sit on that bench,' he commanded. 'I'll get the car and drive you down so you can oversee the operation.'

'You don't—'

'Just don't argue, Mel,' he advised impatiently, and strode away.

Five minutes later he drove down in MEL 1, with Mrs Bedwell in the back seat. He helped her in and they continued on to the stables, where Mel had a fond reunion with Rimfire before his transfer to the paddock.

'I find this hard to believe,' Etienne said, as they

watched Rimfire follow Mrs Bedwell like a lamb on a loose lead.

Mel smiled inwardly while she observed gravely, 'Most men would.'

He looked down at her, balanced beside him against the fence. 'You believe we have large egos, men in general?'

'Uh…sometimes.'

'You can be honest, Mel.'

She glanced up and her eyes were full of humour. 'All right, often!'

'You could be right. Do you reckon we should transfer the pony over as well?'

'I'd be happier if you did. They're good friends, although Tosh might have some trouble catching him.'

'Do him good, might take his mind off mischief. Uh…think I could handle the pony?'

She laughed outright. 'I'm sure your ego isn't that bruised, Etienne!'

'How would you know?' he asked with his eyes alight with devilry, and went away.

The pony, in fact, was delighted to join Rimfire in the paddock and presented no problem to Etienne. And he stopped briefly to converse with Mrs Bedwell before returning to Mel and helping her up into the Range Rover.

She looked a question at him as he started up, and Mrs Bedwell waved to them.

'She's going to walk back to the house. I thought you might like a tour of the property; no walking, but at least you can look.'

A delighted smile spread over Mel's face. 'I would *love* to!'

He grimaced. 'You're easily pleased.'

So that was what they did. Inspected the cattle, the state of the pineapple crop, two crucial dams on the property and the state of her free-range chickens.

And for the first time Mel saw fences where they'd been rather desperately needed, a new roof on the shed where the pineapples were stored and a brand-new tractor.

'Oh, wow!' she said, feasting her eyes on the shiny mechanical marvel. 'What a beauty! When did that arrive?'

'Only a day or so ago. I forgot to mention it. I've also employed a couple of new hands, as we did discuss before we got married.'

'I'm not going to take issue with any of it,' she told him with a wry little smile. 'We needed them *before* I got taken out of action.'

They were driving slowly up the drive now in late-afternoon sunlight. Insects were hovering in the clear air and there was a golden glow over the paddocks.

'So, am I forgiven?' Etienne asked.

'For what?' She raised her eyebrows at him.

'Being a bit tough on you earlier.' He swung the wheel and brought the car to a halt in front of the main steps.

She sighed, but contentedly. 'You are!'

He slid his arm along her backrest and looked down at her rather probingly.

She blinked a couple of times. 'What?'

'Nothing.' He looked away and went to open his door.

'Etienne.' She waited until he turned back. 'Thank
you, for everything.'

'My pleasure, ma'am.' This time he got out and
came around to get her. He lifted her out and carried
her into the house, and his strength and his warmth,
all of which she craved but for some reason was being
denied, assaulted Mel again.

The second instance that broke the peace of those
three weeks was not of her doing. Etienne invited his
second-in-command, Roger Mason, and his wife Sue,
for a late-afternoon barbecue one Sunday. He explained to Mel that he'd asked them because it would
help her to get to know them before the dinner party.
Not only that but it also showed her another side of
Etienne.

He gave Mrs Bedwell the whole weekend off; he
took over the kitchen and press-ganged the boys into
helping him.

For the barbecue, Justin had charge of the fire,
Ewan was the drinks waiter and Tosh became
Etienne's offsider. The boys seemed to enjoy this and
were all spruced up without any of the usual com-
plaints.

It was a glorious afternoon on Sunday. The barbecue was on the east lawn; there was a long wooden
table beside it and some comfortable recliners. Mel
was commanded to relax and talk to the guests while
Etienne put the finishing touches to his preparations.

'We were devastated to miss your wedding,' Roger
Mason said on being introduced, 'weren't we, Susie?'
He was about fifty and short but with humorous eyes.

'We certainly were,' his wife, who looked to be the

same age but was half a head taller, agreed, 'but we were overseas. I believe it was a lovely day, though.'

Mel was saved from replying because at that point the Masons handed her a wedding gift which, when opened, proved to be a set of three beautifully carved mahogany horses on an inlaid brass plinth.

'Oh, how lovely!' She was genuinely thrilled and moved. 'Thank you so much! But how did you know I love horses?'

'A little bird told us!' Susie Mason winked at her.

They sat down and began to chat easily. Mel was persuaded to tell them all about Rimfire and how she was coping with her crutches and in return she learnt that Susie and Roger were mad about pigs, which they raised as a hobby on their smallholding.

So it was all going really well, when Susie looked around and said enthusiastically, 'This is so lovely! Have you always lived here, Mel?'

'Yes, I have.'

'It's why she married Etienne,' Tosh confided as he offered a plate of snacks around. 'So she could go on living here, so we all could, I guess. We couldn't have afforded it otherwise.'

'It was *not*,' Ewan muttered with a furious glance in Tosh's direction as he was about to top up Roger's wine.

'But I heard you and Justin talking about it!' Tosh objected. 'That's what *was said*.'

Ewan slammed his bottle of wine down on the table and tackled his younger brother around the legs, yelling, at the same time as cocktail sausages, pieces of cheese and olives flew everywhere, 'You have got to be the most *infuriating* kid ever invented!'

'Whoa!' It was Etienne, coming down the steps with dishes of meat and kebabs in his hands. 'What have we here?' He put everything down and deftly grabbed a boy in each hand. Tosh came up for air, red-faced and supremely indignant, whilst Ewan still looked to be fighting mad.

'OK, here's what I suggest,' Etienne said easily but with an undertone of command, 'you both apologise, the mess gets cleared up and we have no more of this.'

'But…' It was Tosh, of course.

'Now, Tosh.'

Tosh looked up at his brother-in-law and for once in his life what he saw persuaded him to desist. It must have communicated itself to Ewan as well because both boys mumbled their apologies and began to clean up.

'What was that all about?'

They'd just waved the Masons off. Thanks to the social skills of Etienne and their guests, the barbecue had proceeded as if nothing had happened.

Mel had turned to go indoors but she turned back slowly and explained briefly. 'Tosh…I guess his only mistake was telling it as he'd overheard it being told, and a supreme lack of discretion, but he is only ten,' she finished.

Etienne was leaning against a post, laughing silently.

'I agree that in all other circumstances it could have been funny,' she said carefully.

He straightened. 'I wonder where he gets it from?'

'Me,' she returned flatly.

'Mel.' He sobered and looked at her narrowly, then paused.

She shrugged. 'If you don't mind everyone knowing how it happened, who am I to quibble? It's the truth anyway.'

Something flickered in his gaze. 'I can guarantee no one will hear anything from the Masons; they're far too nice.'

She lifted her chin at him. 'It's bound to get out sooner or later.'

'What exactly is bothering you, Mel?' he asked dangerously.

She gazed at him then turned to hop away.

'No. Hang on.' He put a hand on her shoulder. 'I would have thought everything was going well. We seem to be integrating with no problems, the farm is coming good, your leg is healing properly as the last lot of X-rays showed—and it's no one else's damn business anyway.'

'Then, as you say, everything is fine, Etienne,' she murmured. 'May I go?'

He swore. 'Don't tell me you're turning out like every other bloody woman on the planet?'

He now had her pinned against the wall of the house and she could feel not only the full force of his exasperation but also all the things that drove her a little crazy about him. The power of his tall frame, the heady scent of pure man, his hands that she loved and sometimes couldn't look at without remembering them on her body before he'd stopped touching her in a certain way.

'What do you…mean?' she stammered.

'I mean,' he said through his teeth, 'the way

women specialise in making it clear they have a grievance but refuse to articulate it.'

Her heart was hammering uncomfortably but the injustice of this was too much in that this was no ordinary grievance surely?

'*Are* we all the same?' she asked. 'Or would you rather I was like Paula Littleby and told the whole world?'

'No. I'd rather you told *me*.'

'I don't think this is a very good idea, that's all,' she said at last.

'When did you ever, Mel?' His eyes bored into hers.

'I mean—I don't mean us getting married.' She swallowed.

He was dead still for a moment then appeared to tone down his exasperation a notch. 'What, then?'

'I don't think we should argue in front—'

'In front of the kids?' His gaze was withering but he did look around then. 'There's not a one in sight,' he added sardonically, however.

'That doesn't mean to say—'

'How right you are if you mean the walls have ears. OK. If you would just tell me what's really bothering you,' he went on more normally, 'maybe I can fix it.'

'Etienne,' she drew a deep breath, 'I'm sorry. I've probably made a mountain out of a molehill but it was highly embarrassing at the time. Not only that but also I hate to think of Tosh being confused and Ewan being embarrassed about it all.'

'They've probably put it all behind them by now. Are you sure that's it?'

'Yes.'

He observed her critically then frowned. 'You know, I would have thought this time for you,' he gestured down towards her leg, 'would have been the perfect opportunity for you to really get to work on one of your beloved causes.'

'I—' She hesitated. 'After the debacle of the Littlebys, I wondered if I do rush in where angels fear to tread so I decided to re-evaluate my...thinking a bit.'

'Blow the Littlebys,' he said roughly. 'Don't you dare change there either.'

'How else have I changed?'

He paused. 'You used to—tell me everything.'

'Did I?' she asked with some irony.

He shrugged. 'I clearly recall all the ups and downs of your wedding day.'

'But when I tried to explain why I was having reservations about us, you—weren't that impressed.'

He ignored the last bit and pounced on the first bit of her comment. 'So those reservations are still there?'

'I don't know.' She hesitated. 'Things have changed so much because of this.' She looked down at her cast.

'Things had to change.'

'Yes. Of course.'

'We seem to be going round in circles here,' he said slowly.

She cleared her throat. 'Sorry. My fault, I guess. My sense of humour may have got a bit battered along with my leg.'

He smiled slightly. 'I didn't realise Ewan had such a temper.'

'He doesn't lose it often but when he does...' She shrugged.

Justin came out onto the veranda and Etienne moved away from Mel. 'He's right, though,' he said with a grin. 'Tosh has all the tact of a tank. I've just come to report that they're talking to each other again.'

And so the situation defused itself. Beyond a searching look at her, Etienne made no further comment then or later.

'Mrs B,' Mel said on the afternoon of the dinner party, 'if you wanted to look particularly stunning, would you wear this or this?'

Two outfits from her first consignment of designer clothes lay on her bed.

'Well, now.' Mrs Bedwell studied the two outfits, a long black dress with a square neckline, and a gorgeous white linen blouse with a floral skirt with lace inserts. 'I have no idea! You'll have to try them on.'

'That—is not so easy! Anyway, anything I wear is going to look ridiculous,' Mel added with sudden despair.

Mrs Bedwell cast her a narrow little look. 'Honey,' she said, 'that's just not true—'

'But—'

'No, listen to me, Mel! Everything is under control. The table looks wonderful; trust me, the food will have them in transports! And I still believe all you have to do is be yourself.'

Mel was sitting on the bed next to her new clothes, and she took a deep breath.

'I'll help you try them on,' Mrs Bedwell added.

Half an hour later, she made her choice. 'The blouse and skirt. You look more comfortable in them, you look young and lovely!'

Mel picked up the white linen blouse. It had cap sleeves, a keyhole opening below the neckline and a broad lace insert above the waist then a peplum that covered the top of the skirt.

'I did feel comfortable in it,' she agreed, 'but not that sophisticated.' She eyed the black dress.

'The cast seems to be more noticeable against the black; not only that, it may not be a good idea to try for too much sophistication,' Mrs Bedwell said shrewdly, 'with a broken leg.'

'You're right,' Mel agreed ruefully. 'OK, will you help me wash my hair?'

'Sure thing!'

Several hours later all was ready, the guests were due shortly, the old house looked wonderful and the boys had all gone to spend the night with friends.

Mel was dressed and ready and quite pleased with what she saw. She'd even experimented in front of the mirror and decided that her blouse was rather tantalising. The keyhole opening gave subtle glimpses of her breasts as she moved. Would it tantalise Etienne? she wondered. Would it cause him to want to rip it off her? What would it be like to have him touch her breasts and kiss them?

She closed her eyes and sighed. What was the point of fantasising? What was the point of—anything any more? And she suddenly found herself unable to leave her room.

Then the door clicked open and Etienne stood there

with two glasses in his hands. She'd seen him when he'd come home from work then they'd both gone to get changed—she with Mrs Bedwell's help and a relayed invitation to join Etienne in the lounge when she was dressed.

'I was coming,' she lied, from the depths of the armchair.

'Sure.' He put a glass in her hand and a little box in her lap. 'By the way, Roger Mason had to go home because of an abscess on a tooth so his son David is taking his place tonight.'

'Oh! That's thoughtful of them.'

'Yes. You'll probably like him. He's doing architecture at university.'

'What is this?' Mel asked of the drink.

'Brandy. I always like one before any ordeal.' He sat on the end of the bed. His curly hair was tamed and he wore a cream shirt with a charcoal suit and a sage-green tie with topaz elephants on it.

She blinked at the tie. 'That's rather—colourful!'

He squinted down at it. 'It's my good-luck tie.'

'I'm the one who needs good luck tonight, not you!'

'Well, since elephants work for me, I thought they might work for you, Mel. We could be—united in good luck. Open the box.'

She set her drink down and clicked open the box. There was a pair of earrings nestled on the white velvet, little pink elephants with ruby eyes and tiny diamond saddles on delicate gold chains.

'Oh, they're gorgeous!' She looked up, her eyes alight.

'Try them on.'

She did so and swung her head.

He smiled at her obvious pleasure then said gravely, 'I promise, they do work.'

'Elephants?' A tinge of curiosity entered her gaze. 'How come? That you believe in them, I mean?'

'I went to Africa once and got charged by an elephant protecting her calf. It made an indelible impression on me.'

'I would have thought a flattening impression!'

'Oh, I was in a Land-Rover and we managed to move off in time.' He looked wry. 'When I came home, I designed a logo for Hurst Engineering & Shipping that I still use now.' He paused. 'We've gone from strength to strength ever since.'

Mel took a breath. 'You do know the African elephant is in danger of extinction?'

'Yes, Mel. That's why at the bottom of my logo there's a "save the elephant" sign.'

She frowned. 'I've never noticed it!'

'The logo or the sign?'

'Both! That's...very remiss of me, Etienne, and I applaud you!'

'Thank you.' He stood up. 'Finish your drink.'

But she stayed where she was, looking troubled.

'Mel?'

'Etienne, have you changed your mind about being married to me?'

There, it was out at last, she thought, but closed her eyes in despair at her timing.

He paused. 'What makes you think that?'

'I just wondered, that's all,' she murmured.

'I thought I'd explained the situation,' he said.

'So you did.' She reached for her crutches and got up at last. 'OK. I'm ready.'

'Mel,' he looked at her grimly, 'is that what's been worrying you? Why the hell couldn't you have told me sooner?'

She shrugged. 'I don't know.'

He studied her from the top of her head to her toes. Her hair was loose tonight although tucked behind her ears. Her eyes were like deep blue pansies and despite the cast she was lovely, achingly lovely, but so— untouched and innocent, he thought.

'Whatever happens to this marriage,' he said harshly, 'you, the boys and Raspberry Hill will be safe.'

Mel's heart sank like a stone. 'What does that mean?' she whispered with her eyes widening.

'It means I'd set up a trust if necessary—and please don't start on about charity.' He looked at her drily and someone knocked on the door.

It was Mrs Bedwell with the news that the first car was coming up the drive.

'We're coming,' Etienne said without turning his head.

'I can't!' Mel said in sudden panic.

'Yes, you can. It was all your idea anyway.' He walked to the door and held it open for her.

'And now I know why you weren't too keen on it,' she retorted.

His hand closed on her wrist like a vice, then he swore as they heard Mrs Bedwell welcoming the Masons.

'Afterwards,' he said, and she had no doubt it was a threat.

CHAPTER TWELVE

THERE was not one glitch during the evening.

The Malaysian couples spoke beautiful English and were delighted to be in a private home. The wife of the RSPCA president was delighted to meet some of her compatriots. The mayor and his wife were either suffering from diplomatic or genuine memory loss but they made no mention of the Rimfire incident and obviously enjoyed themselves. The Masons, mother and son, were invaluable—and Sue Mason made no mention of the Tosh-Ewan debacle.

Mrs Bedwell excelled herself, the food was inspired, and Mel felt that in a quiet way she'd played the role of hostess well.

Moreover, thanks to Etienne's social skills, no one would have guessed that they were in the middle of a domestic dispute.

Though unexpected assistance came to Mel from David Mason. She guessed he was about twenty-two, he was fair and of medium height with hazel eyes, and he was also articulate and humorous. Without appearing to try he made her laugh, and they discovered they were both horse mad.

Not that anything could make her forget the shadow over her life but David Mason's wit and, if she was honest, his open admiration of her helped her get through the evening.

But all too soon the dinner party was over and she

and Etienne were farewelling their guests side by side at the top of the veranda steps.

As the last car drove off, her nerves tightened and her fingers on the bars of her crutches whitened.

'So,' he said and loosened his tie, 'a successful evening?'

'I think so.'

'Then what reason, other than the obvious, would I have had for not wanting you to hold it?'

She glanced up at him nervously, trying to gauge his mood, to encounter a narrowed and darkly probing look.

She licked her lips. 'If you don't intend to stay married to me, Etienne, it's probably insensitive if nothing else to parade me around as your wife.'

'And would you recommend that I stay married to a wife who really doesn't want me?' he drawled.

Mel took a ragged breath. 'I haven't said that.'

'Let's not beat about the bush—you haven't exactly welcomed this marriage other than for the purpose of providing for your brothers and saving this place.'

The cool night air drew a shiver from her, but it wasn't only the night air that made her feel chilled to the bone.

'Etienne,' she said quietly, 'I shouldn't have married you, I'm sorry. But I must point out that you don't really want me. I mean—'

However, before she could go any further, Batman, newly released by Mrs Bedwell from his incarceration in the laundry, raced out onto the veranda like a streak of lightning. At the same time Mel, desperately concentrating on trying to make sense to Etienne, was

taken so much by surprise she moved convulsively,
lost her footing and toppled down the front steps.

Etienne tried to catch her but, in the mêlée of dog
and crutches, he didn't succeed. He scrambled down
the steps. 'Mel—*Mel*? Are you all right? For heaven's
sake, Mel—Batman, get *lost*!' He shoved the dog
away and sat down beside her to pull her into his
arms. 'Mel? My love,' he said into her hair, 'tell me
you're OK? Your leg…?'

Mel opened her eyes; the fall had winded her
briefly, but she wondered if she'd lost consciousness
because she couldn't believe what she was hearing.

'What did you say?' she whispered.

'Your leg? And all your other bones—how do they
feel?'

'I don't know yet, but I meant—before that, what
did you say?'

'I can't remember,' he said distractedly, now running his hands cautiously over her. 'Why the hell am
I so accident-prone when you're with me?'

'It wasn't you, it was Batman. And it wasn't you
before, it was a rock and a tree.'

'All the same, I hardly have a good record of keeping you safe and sound. Listen, let's try and get you
up.'

Two minutes later, she was standing on one foot
and he was holding her around her waist. 'What do
you think?' He scanned her face for any signs of pain.

'I think I'm OK,' she said cautiously. 'I might have
a few bruises, that's all.' Nevertheless, she suddenly
burst into tears.

He swore beneath his breath, picked her up in his
arms and carried her inside to her bedroom. On the

way he encountered Mrs Bedwell looking wildly curious and apprehensive but he shook his head at her.

Once he'd laid Mel on her bed, propped against some pillows, he closed the door before coming back to the bed. 'Tell me where it hurts,' he said gently.

She wiped her face but the tears kept coming. 'For a moment there I thought you'd called me your love but I must have been m-mistaken; that's what hurts,' she wept. 'Otherwise I'm fine.'

'Mel,' he sat down on the side of the bed with a frown in his eyes, 'isn't that the last thing you'd want to hear?'

'No! I've been so lost and lonely since the accident because I thought it might have happened for you as it had happened for me but it obviously hadn't.'

'It did happen,' he said grimly. 'Only it made me see the error of my ways, I guess.'

'What error of your ways?' At last, the tears subsided and she stared at him with streaks of mascara down her face.

He leant forward and smudged them. 'What error?' he said with harsh lines scored beside his mouth. 'How about forcing you to marry me?'

Her lips parted.

'How about being quite sure that once I got you into my bed all your reservations would melt?'

'Etienne—'

'How about having to have Jim Dalton make me stop and think of you as a person who was a lot more mature than I ever gave you credit for?'

'Is that—is that what Jim did?'

'He also warned me against hurting you,' he said

drily, 'but you see, Mel, not only did I underestimate you badly but I was also planning to rob you.'

'I don't see how.' She looked around the chalk-blue bedroom. 'Just about everything I have comes courtesy of you.'

'I'm talking about your youth and your innocence and the fact that you haven't had a chance yet to spread your wings and fall in love; have fun with…someone like David Mason, perhaps.' His eyes were suddenly alert and probing.

'I don't want to fall in love with David Mason. I have already fallen in love, you see. Maybe it didn't happen in a conventional way but it did happen.'

He hesitated. 'What happened at the bottom of the embankment might not be a reliable guide, Mel.'

'It's not only what happened at the bottom of the embankment,' she said. 'I may not have been able to articulate this to myself before the accident and I certainly wasn't able to explain it to you, but my deepest reservation about marrying you, Etienne, was the one to do with me…growing to *love* you…while you only wanted me.'

He let several beats pass.

Before he could say anything, she went on, 'You once said something about going to the ends of the earth for each other. Well, since the accident, since you drew back from me, I've felt as if I've been at the end of the earth, in some cold, lonely, desolate place,' she shuddered, 'and I'm neither too young nor too innocent not to know why.'

'You could have told me this,' he said barely audibly.

'Well, maybe that is one of the problems of being

a bit young and innocent,' she said with a little smile. 'How to tell a man you're not sure of how much you love him—is not in any etiquette book.'

'Not sure of?' he repeated with deep intensity. 'Oh, Mel, I've been trying to tell myself I haven't fallen in love with you since…since the day of the funeral. I couldn't believe it could happen like that for me but it did. Sweetheart,' his eyes searched hers, 'are you sure?'

She sniffed. 'You know me. I don't change my mind.'

'Then are you very sure you're not in any way injured or further injured?' he asked gravely.

'Yes. Why?'

'Because I desperately need to do this.' He lay down beside her and took her in his arms. 'I love you. I've been going crazy these last weeks!'

Mel breathed ecstatically and ran her fingertips down his face then she stilled and looked stern. 'You hid it well!'

'Think so? I seem to remember calling you a bloody fool and accusing you of being like every other woman on the planet, whereas one of the things I love about you is that you're not like any other woman I know.'

'You said…you said something like that to me once before,' she marvelled. 'I didn't know what to make of it at the time.'

'Did I?' He stroked her hair.

'Yes. When you asked me to marry you, I said something about most girls jumping at the chance but I wasn't most girls. You said you wouldn't be asking me if I were.'

'Do you believe me now?'

She snuggled up against him. 'I feel as if I've come home.'

He started to kiss her.

Until she said huskily, as she quivered finely all over at what his hands and mouth were doing to her, 'Etienne, what are we going to do? It's another five weeks before the cast comes off.'

He lifted his head. 'Do you trust me, Mel?'

'After what you did for me when I broke my leg, I'd trust you with my life but—'

'It can be done.'

Her eyes widened. 'You said—'

'It's what I tried to tell myself.' He grimaced. 'But I actually got medical advice that, with great care, of course, it's now possible.'

'You did that? Why? I mean, if you weren't planning to make love to me—'

'I wasn't sure I could trust myself.'

She laughed softly.

He raised an eyebrow at her. 'That appeals to you?'

'I don't know why but it does!'

'So you're not as prim and proper as you gave me to understand?' he queried, his eyes alight with devilry.

'It seems—not in relation to you, Etienne,' she agreed gravely. 'I have had,' she stopped and blushed, 'well, some astonishing fantasies about you.'

'Tell me.'

'Uh—one day, maybe.'

'At least give me an idea of how you'd like me to begin.'

She thought for a bit. 'By taking my clothes off?'

'Ah.' He sat up. 'That's actually a basic require-
ment in these circumstances. Moreover,' he glinted a
wicked look into her eyes, 'this damn keyhole in your
blouse has been driving me mad.'

Mel sat up and squinted down at her blouse. 'You
know, I was hoping it might.'

He looked comically put out. 'Does that mean you
plan to make a habit of tantalising the life out of me?'

'I might.'

'I have to tell you,' he said sternly, 'I *love* the
sound of that.' He drew her into his arms and started
to kiss her again.

Then, item by item, he started to undress her and
himself. He took his jacket and elephant tie off and
turned his attention to the offending blouse. It came
off, then his shirt, and, with exquisite attention to de-
tail, he caressed every inch of her upper body before
he released her bra and consigned it to the floor.

'Nice?' he asked as he cupped her breasts and
touched her nipples.

Mel was breathing slowly and deeply, visibly affected, and she slipped her hands around his neck so
their foreheads were touching. 'Perfect,' she murmured. She took her hands from his neck and covered
his hands over her breasts. 'I wondered, quite recently, what it would be like if you kissed them.'

'Let's find out.'

She tilted her head back but it was her throat he
kissed and her shoulders while he stroked the soft skin
down her sides. But each butterfly kiss was a prelude
to almost unbearable pleasure as her nipples peaked
in anticipation of what he would do to them.

She gasped and writhed beneath his hands as the moment came. 'That's...I can't tell you...'

'And I can't tell you what it's doing to me,' he growled. 'Permission to proceed?'

'Yes, oh, yes!'

They shed the rest of their clothes without taking their eyes off each other and with frequent interruptions for touching, experimenting, tasting...

So that losing her virginity came to Mel as the most natural, wonderful thing in the world beneath his guidance and his care not to hurt her despite his obvious need of her. It came like a *bel canto* experience of exquisite purity and artistry that took her breath away and left her so much more in love with Etienne Hurst, she was unable to speak or move for an age.

'How did that affect your broken leg?' he said at last, cradling her to him as if he'd never let her go.

'What broken leg?' she said dreamily.

He grinned. 'Good.'

'I *love* you.' She moved her cheek against his shoulder. 'I thought I did before but now it's worse.'

'Worse?'

'Yes,' she assured him and moved as one of her earrings dug into her neck. 'Oh! I forgot to take my precious elephants off!'

'The bride wore her earrings and a plaster cast,' he teased, running his hand down her body.

She looked into his eyes then said humorously, 'You may not know this but I made a pact with myself to be an unconventional bride.'

'Darling, my darling Mel,' he said, and sobered suddenly, 'I love every unconventional inch of you.

But if that pact was made because of the injustices I did you, am I forgiven?'

'So long as you never go away from me again.'

'I won't,' he promised. 'But you haven't told me why it's worse now?'

'Oh,' she ran her fingers through his hair, 'what I meant was that it's even more serious. You're not only the hero of my dreams and fantasies, and they were quite something, but you're also the hero of my reality now.'

'Quite something,' he repeated. 'Listen, before I die of curiosity, I think you'd better tell me about these fantasies.'

'Not all at once.'

'Pick one, then,' he suggested.

'Well,' she sat up, 'you may not recall her but there was a girl in a filmy, silvery dress who floated over a lawn towards you one day—'

'A girl with chestnut hair and deep blue eyes?' he queried.

'Yes. She also had a cheetah cub with a jewelled collar—sapphires, rubies and emeralds.'

His eyes widened. 'Not a Jack Russell puppy?'

'No,' Mel said gravely. 'Definitely not. There was absolutely nothing mundane about this girl. She wasn't intimidated, she wasn't unsure of herself, she was a free spirit entirely.'

'So—what did she do?'

'She took your hand, she pulled you down to the grass, and I have to tell you, Etienne, you have no idea how close you came to being—ravished.'

'*Ravished?*' He sat up beside her.

She looked at him gravely. 'I hope you don't disapprove?'

'On the contrary—would this have been the day you agreed to marry me by any chance?'

She nodded then started to laugh. 'Don't ask me *where* she came from and *why* she needed to have a cheetah cub—'

'I won't.' He pulled her into his arms and lay back with her. 'I'll concentrate on the "being ravished" bit.' He drew his hand down the curve of her breast and the flare of her hip.

'Those details are a little hazy,' she revealed, as a tremor of desire ran through her.

'Maybe I can help there?' He smiled lazily.

'Oh?'

'Mmm… Close your eyes.'

She did so and his hands moved on her in a way that caused her heart rate to triple until she murmured unsteadily with her eyes still shut. 'Just who…is ravishing whom?'

'If I'm ravishing you,' he said, 'it's only because I'm utterly ravished at the prospect of spending the rest of my life married to you—and all the other versions of you.'

Her lashes flew up. 'Wait until you hear about the naked wood nymph and the concubine.'

He groaned. 'I mightn't survive!'

But she assured him he would, and when they stopped laughing, some wonderful, mutual ravishment took place.

The world's bestselling romance series.

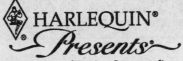

Seduction and Passion Guaranteed!

They're guaranteed to raise your pulse!

Meet the most eligible medical men of the world, in a new series of stories, by popular authors, that will make your heart race!

Whether they're saving lives or dealing with desire, our doctors have got bedside manners that send temperatures soaring....

Coming in Harlequin Presents in 2003:

THE DOCTOR'S SECRET CHILD by Catherine Spencer
#2311, on sale March

THE PASSION TREATMENT by Kim Lawrence
#2330, on sale June

THE DOCTOR'S RUNAWAY BRIDE by Sarah Morgan
#2366, on sale December

Pick up a Harlequin Presents® novel and you will enter a world of spine-tingling passion and provocative, tantalizing romance!

Available wherever Harlequin books are sold.

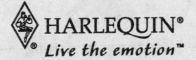

Visit us at www.eHarlequin.com

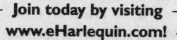

Your opinion is important to us! Please take a few moments to share your thoughts with us about your experiences with Harlequin and Silhouette books. Your comments will be very useful in ensuring that we deliver books you love to read.
Please take a few minutes to complete the questionnaire, then send it to us at the address below.

Send your completed questionnaires to:
Harlequin/Silhouette Reader Survey, P.O. Box 9046, Buffalo, NY 14269-9046

1. As you may know, there are many different lines under the Harlequin and Silhouette brands. Each of the lines is listed below. Please check the box that most represents your reading habit for each line.

Line	Currently read this line	Do not read this line	Not sure if I read this line
Harlequin American Romance	❏	❏	❏
Harlequin Duets	❏	❏	❏
Harlequin Romance	❏	❏	❏
Harlequin Historicals	❏	❏	❏
Harlequin Superromance	❏	❏	❏
Harlequin Intrigue	❏	❏	❏
Harlequin Presents	❏	❏	❏
Harlequin Temptation	❏	❏	❏
Harlequin Blaze	❏	❏	❏
Silhouette Special Edition	❏	❏	❏
Silhouette Romance	❏	❏	❏
Silhouette Intimate Moments	❏	❏	❏
Silhouette Desire	❏	❏	❏

2. Which of the following best describes why you bought *this book?* One answer only, please.

the picture on the cover ❏ the title ❏
the author ❏ the line is one I read often ❏
part of a miniseries ❏ saw an ad in another book ❏
saw an ad in a magazine/newsletter ❏ a friend told me about it ❏
I borrowed/was given this book ❏ other: _____ ❏

3. Where did you buy *this book?* One answer only, please.

at Barnes & Noble ❏ at a grocery store ❏
at Waldenbooks ❏ at a drugstore ❏
at Borders ❏ on eHarlequin.com Web site ❏
at another bookstore ❏ from another Web site ❏
at Wal-Mart ❏ Harlequin/Silhouette Reader ❏
at Target ❏ Service/through the mail
at Kmart ❏ used books from anywhere ❏
at another department store ❏ I borrowed/was given this ❏
or mass merchandiser book

4. On average, how many Harlequin and Silhouette books do you buy at one time?

I buy _____ books at one time ❏
I rarely buy a book ❏

MRQ403HP-1A

5. How many times per month do you shop for any *Harlequin and/or Silhouette* books?
   One answer only, please.

1 or more times a week	❑	a few times per year	❑
1 to 3 times per month	❑	less often than once a year	❑
1 to 2 times every 3 months	❑	never	❑

6. When you think of your ideal heroine, which *one* statement describes her the best?
   One answer only, please.

She's a woman who is strong-willed	❑	She's a desirable woman	❑
She's a woman who is needed by others	❑	She's a powerful woman	❑
She's a woman who is taken care of	❑	She's a passionate woman	❑
She's an adventurous woman	❑	She's a sensitive woman	❑

7. The following statements describe types or genres of books that you may be
   interested in reading. Pick *up to 2 types* of books that you are most interested in.

   I like to read about truly romantic relationships ❑
   I like to read stories that are sexy romances ❑
   I like to read romantic comedies ❑
   I like to read a romantic mystery/suspense ❑
   I like to read about romantic adventures ❑
   I like to read romance stories that involve family ❑
   I like to read about a romance in times or places that I have never seen ❑
   Other: _____ ❑

*The following questions help us to group your answers with those readers who are
similar to you. Your answers will remain confidential.*

8. Please record your year of birth below.

   19 _____

9. What is your marital status?

   single ❑   married ❑   common-law ❑   widowed ❑
   divorced/separated ❑

10. Do you have children 18 years of age or younger currently living at home?

    yes ❑   no ❑

11. Which of the following best describes your employment status?

    employed full-time or part-time ❑   homemaker ❑   student ❑
    retired ❑   unemployed ❑

12. Do you have access to the Internet from either home or work?

    yes ❑   no ❑

13. Have you ever visited eHarlequin.com?

    yes ❑   no ❑

14. What state do you live in?

    _____

15. Are you a member of Harlequin/Silhouette Reader Service?

    yes ❑   Account # _____   no ❑   MRQ403HP-1B

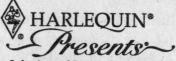

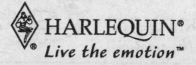

HARLEQUIN *Super*ROMANCE®

New York Times bestselling author

DEBBIE MACOMBER

brings you a brand-new and long-awaited book
featuring three of her most popular characters—
the matchmaking and always mischievous
angels Shirley, Goodness and Mercy.
And she brings it to Superromance!

THOSE CHRISTMAS ANGELS

Available in November,
wherever Harlequin books are sold.